a mother's gift

barb reimer

A Mother's Gift

First Edition Published by Brimstone Ink 2021
Calgary, Alberta
Second Edition Published by Brimstone Ink 2023
Diamond Valley, Alberta
Copyright ⊆ 2021 by Barb Reimer

This is a work of fiction and is solely the product of the author's imagination. Neither the characters nor their names are connected to anyone with the same or similar name, except where obvious and then only in homage to that person. Likewise, business and events are fictional. Some locations in the story are real but used in a way that is purely fictional and for atmospheric purposes. Any resemblance to real people or events, or places is coincidental.

Cover Art by Book Brush and Tawny Nina at Pixabay

ISBN 978-1-777-6155-1-2 (paperback)
978-1-777-6155-0-5 (e-book)

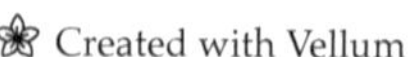 Created with Vellum

This book is for the women of my heritage –
Anna, Ilma, Ellen, Alice Sr., and Alice Jr., Shirley, and Linda.
You taught me indirectly and directly about being brave and steady
despite the circumstances, working hard yet remembering to have
fun, and spreading kindness and joy in your wake.

To the cast of women in my life today –
Kathy, Jamie, Paisley, Lily, and Kenzie.
I am proud that you already show these traits. You are the next
generation of our long line of incredible women.

one

. . .

CHARLOTTE MARTIN STOOD in front of the mirror like she had every day since she started working. This is where she contemplated the day before driving to the office. However, this morning was different. Today she dressed in her best suit. She'd bought it for the president's visit last month, to impress him, to show she wanted to be seen as a serious professional. She wasn't sure it had made any impression at all. Then, yesterday, an appointment with her boss appeared on her calendar. There could be no other reason than to discuss a promotion. She was an excellent accountant. Charlotte always met her deadlines and accurately completed her work. She was sure it was her turn because others hired after her were already managers.

A promotion would prove that she was a success. *Work hard and do excellent work. Get promoted. Become a boss.* Those words, drilled into her head by her mother, were Irene's definition of success, even though Irene had never held a job. Irene's definitions had guided Charlotte all her life. But she still wasn't successful in her mother's eyes. Irene told Charlotte she would never be good enough to be a manager, she wasn't pretty enough to find a husband, and she was too smart for anyone to take any interest in her. Well, starting today, Charlotte was going to show her mother just how wrong she was, at least about work. This new job was the key.

Charlotte shook her head, refusing to let her mother's voice in that morning. Today she would arrive at the office, get noticed because she looked good, and at ten o'clock, sit in the office of her boss, and hear what she had been waiting to hear for the past three years. That she was now a manager.

Charlotte took the job at the firm after graduating from university. They told her at the interview they liked her top marks and the references from her summer work. Charlotte felt she had not disappointed them. The firm's clients often expressed how impressed they were with her work, and she watched her boss strut at the praise. She tried to ignore that he acted as if it was for him and not the firm or her work.

Today, all the late nights and weekends would give her the reward she desired. It didn't matter that she didn't have a social life. It didn't matter that she lived with her mother in a basement suite and drove an older car. It only mattered that she would be a manager. And then her life could change. For the better.

She was giddy with excitement. Her reflection smiled at her as she took one more look at her appearance. The suit was not as modern as the labels worn by others in the firm. A black elastic ponytail holder tied back her long honey-brown hair and her glasses were the style popular about five years ago. Her face didn't have any glow, it was always serene and unexpressive. Not quite a smile, but not quite a frown. She didn't exercise regularly, like the others in the office who spent their free time in the gym or hiking. She wasn't fat, but she certainly was curvier than the skinny stick people at work.

Charlotte left her basement suite to get to her car parked behind the back fence. Charlotte and Peewee, the neighbor's German Shepherd, had an adversarial relationship—he barked without stopping every time he saw her and lunged at her when she got near the fence. She could only avoid an interaction with him if she walked to the front of the house. His ferocity made Charlotte keep an eye on him and her heart race because one day he had escaped his yard and chased her. Luckily, she had beaten the dog to her car and was able to slam the door in its face. The wooden fence between her house and the neighbors was rickety and had some loose boards. Charlotte had asked the neighbors to fix their fence, but their solution had been to nail a couple of extra boards to the posts. The dog had already pawed at and chewed a hole in these.

Today, she wasn't paying any attention to Peewee. Her mind was occupied by the meeting and how her life would change. Charlotte got into the ancient two door Toyota Celica she had had since university. It was used when she bought it, but it had been reliable and got her to work and back. It would be the second thing she'd replace. Where she lived would be first.

Charlotte shared a home with her mother. It was a house with a suite in the basement. Charlotte lived in the suite. Her mother lived in the rest of the house. This arrangement had been made when her dad had to be moved to the care facility. It was intended to be temporary, but so far temporary had lasted six years. Irene didn't work, which made Charlotte's job all that more important. She supported her mother, which didn't leave her much money for fun. The promotion would change that. Charlotte tried not to think about how much she wanted to move to her own home. It was something she'd thought of every day for the last six years.

With no job and few friends, Irene met Charlotte at the door every night and badgered her about everything.

"Did you wear that to work today? Wrong choice."

"What did you eat for lunch?"

"Is your rent money in the bank?"

"You were out late last night."

Charlotte felt like she was twelve, didn't make good choices, and couldn't do anything that pleased Irene. It had been like that all her life but felt harder to take since her dad had passed. Charlotte was sure that if Irene had a job, it would give her mother something else to do and to think about. For Charlotte, it would take off some of the financial pressure.

She took a deep breath, like she always did where her mother was concerned, and parked her car. She made tea in the kitchen of the office and dug her nose into the work at her desk. It was interesting to review the finances of organizations and figure out how they worked and where they could improve. She often mused if she got paid for opportunities she found to increase their bottom line, she would have been in her own apartment long ago. Engrossed in her work, she missed the hushed voices and the office doors closing and opening.

The next time she looked at her watch, it was just before ten. In the washroom, she checked her face in the mirror, tucked the loose strands of her hair back into place, washed her hands, and returned to her cubicle. She took a deep breath and headed to the tenth floor where her boss sat.

His secretary ushered her into the empty office and offered her water.

"No thanks." Charlotte liked the secretary. She was efficient and not inclined to gossip like the other assistants.

"He'll be here shortly."

Alone, Charlotte took in the accoutrements of her boss' office. A padded chair behind the desk was covered in dark leather. The desk was much larger than her own and only had a few items on it, despite its size. A yellow pad of lined paper sat in the center with two pens and a mechanical pencil lined up beside it. A coffee mug with the words *Big Boss* in gold letters sat next to the phone. There were three books on one corner, an old accounting text that Charlotte recognized from university, and two popular self-improvement books Charlotte had never read. Two large windows framed the river to the east of the city. Charlotte wondered how he got anything done with such a view. She would spend all her time looking out the window if this was her office.

An office like this was something she could look forward to someday. As a manager, she would sit in an inside office and have a door. The corner office with windows would come at the next level. Her mother would be so proud of her then.

The door opened. Charlotte rose to shake her boss' hand and sat back down.

"Charlotte, thanks for meeting with me this morning."

"You're welcome."

"I called this meeting to discuss changes in the organization."

Charlotte's forehead creased. He didn't use the word promotion.

"Our firm is shifting its priorities and reconsidering some of our portfolios so that we can concentrate on a more centralized offering to our clients."

He still didn't say promotion.

"One section we are disbanding is your department."

Her legs started shaking.

"Which means ..." he paused, as if unsure what to say next, "that we will no longer need your services. We have made you redundant." He finished the sentence quickly, as if spitting it out would make it easier to say.

"I'm sorry?" Charlotte's forehead creased more. "Made redundant?" Charlotte barely got the words out. Tears welled in her eyes, and she gripped the chair to control her distress. She focused on her breath, keeping it steady as she tried to understand what was happening.

Her boss did not respond sympathetically to her reaction. "Oh, that's my British side coming out." He laughed as if it was funny. "Your services are no longer required. We are letting you go."

Charlotte swallowed the bile that was coming up her throat. "You mean I'm not being promoted?"

"What? No. You are being let go. There is no longer a job here for you."

Charlotte swallowed the bile again. She didn't know what to think. Then her head was a traffic jam of thoughts.

"But I have worked hard here. The clients have appreciated my work. It was time for my promotion." Words tumbled out of her mouth like the water over a waterfall.

"This is really hard for me, Charlotte."

She heard those words and widened her eyes to a stare. She thought, *Well, imagine how hard this is for me.* But she didn't have the courage to say the words.

"Someone from HR will go over the package." He walked out of the room.

Charlotte hadn't heard his office door open. The HR reps lowered themselves into chairs opposite Charlotte and one pulled out some pages from an envelope. The next minutes were a blur as the package was reviewed. Charlotte was allowed to go to her desk to clear her personal items. She saw other people's eyes lower as she was escorted to the elevator.

"Goodbye, Charlotte," said her escort. "There is a contact number in that envelope if you have questions." And the elevator door shut.

Charlotte walked to her car, opened the door, and sat in it without starting it. *What am I going to tell Mother?* Her breath was still unsteady. Her complete body shook. It amazed her that she'd made it to her car. She sat up and looked at herself in the mirror. She looked the same, but she knew her life had just changed. And not for the better.

two

. . .

CHARLOTTE REALIZED she was driving and blinked her eyes, wondering where she was going. Surely not home? When the car turned left on Bank Street, she knew exactly where she was headed.

Janine Wood was her oldest friend in the world. Her only friend, really. They met on the first day of junior high school when the teacher asked students to find a partner for a math game. It was grade seven, a new school with many new faces. Both girls sat at the back of their individual rows and shyly looked at each other.

"Will you be my partner?" Janine asked Charlotte.

"Yes," Charlotte said.

Each girl laid out their cards and then they took turns matching. Janine had cards with the numbers, Charlotte had the ones with equations. It turned out they were lightning quick at the game and soon were racing through matching a second time, to see how fast they could get through the set.

The teacher walked by their desks, noticing the girls had their cards in two piles. "Do you need any help, girls?"

"No, teacher. We are done." Charlotte said.

"You are done?"

The girls nodded.

"Well, you can do it again." The teacher walked toward another group.

"We did that already."

She stopped and slowly turned on her heel. "Well, we will have to find other things for you two, won't we?"

From her smile, Charlotte knew they weren't in trouble, and she smiled back. She grinned at Janine, and they shared a giggle, cementing their friendship. They had been best friends for over fifteen years.

Janine was one of the few people in Charlotte's life who had witnessed Irene's other side. The first time, Irene was stomping around, throwing towels and clattering dishes in the kitchen. Charlotte and Janine were in her room. Irene whipped open Charlotte's bedroom door and demanded Charlotte get into the living room and practice piano. Charlotte watched Janine's face for a sign of fear, or an indication she would be soon leaving. But Janine acted as though nothing had happened. When they returned to her bedroom after Charlotte had practiced for a half hour, she apologized to Janine for Irene's behavior.

"Charlotte don't apologize for that. This is all your mother. You have done nothing to make her behave how she does."

Charlotte was surprised at Janine's reaction. It never occurred to her that she wasn't the cause of Irene's behavior.

"Your mother has something wrong with her brain. It doesn't fire like normal brains do."

"How do you know that?"

"Oh, there are a few crazies in the Woods family." Janine laughed. "That's what my grandmother called them. She used to laugh at them when they weren't looking. But she taught me to have empathy and stay out of the way until the tornado spent out its energy. She said not to take it personally. It wasn't about me."

"I'm not sure I can do that."

"I'm not sure you can either."

Charlotte frowned at Janine's comment.

"You've said she has done this since you were a little girl, so it's all you know. You never know what is going to trigger her. You might even think this is her way of showing she cares."

"She does. I know she does."

"She may, but she has a weird way of showing it. The way someone shows you they care is with loving kindness. Words and actions that make you feel ten feet tall and able to do anything. Have you ever felt that way?"

"No," Charlotte had to admit, tears filling her eyes. "Maybe with my dad."

"Oh, Charlotte. I am so sorry. You deserve to be loved by both of your parents." Janine hugged her and Charlotte felt better.

She knew at least someone else was on her side besides her dad. He was always careful about showing kindness toward Charlotte, especially after Irene had exploded. He would find a time and place to tell Charlotte that he knew that Irene didn't intend to be mean.

"Your mother sometimes loses her cool. You have to let her get through it and then everything will be okay," was all he ever said, and did. Now she had Janine to provide Charlotte with a downy feathered place to land. She knew she could lean against her and be safe. Today, after being fired, was certainly one of those times.

She asked her cell phone to dial Janine and listened for the phone to ring.

"Hi there."

"Hey you. How are you doing?"

"Um. Okay. You home for a while?"

"Am I anywhere else? You don't sound good. Are you at work?"

"Well, not really. I'm on my way over."

"Tea's on." The phone clicked.

Janine greeted Charlotte with a hug. "Come on in. I put the good stuff on. Now tell me, what has Irene done now?"

Charlotte sat down on a wooden chair at the table that Janine and her family used for meals, homework, and games. The cushions were cushy and covered with a bright yellow pattern that matched the curtains on the window and the placemats piled on the side of the table for mealtime. She had sat at this table often, always as part of the family, taking in the chaos of family life that was noisy, fun, and loving. They made her feel part of their family. She loved that.

Janine poured the boiling water into the china teapot to let it steep. She piled cookies on a matching plate beside the mugs already on the table. "This is not a time for fancy teacups and saucers. This is mug time." Janine pushed the cookies toward Charlotte.

Charlotte took a bite of dark chocolate and walnuts and let the taste sit in her mouth while she gathered her thoughts.

"Irene has done nothing. It's work. I got let go today." Charlotte swallowed the cookie and slowly raised her eyes to meet Janine's.

"Weren't you up for a promotion? What happened? What did Old Fuzziewig say to you?" Janine had called Charlotte's boss Old Fuzziewig since the first time Charlotte described him. An unimpressive man, with pants that had no form or shape, he wore a bow tie and a suit jacket all the time. They laughed that he had decided what a boss looked like from old black and white movies and wore that uniform every day of his life.

"He said that the company was getting rid of my department and that all of us are let go."

"Just like that?"

"Just like that."

"Well, nuts."

"What will my mother say? She'll have a fit when she hears I lost my job."

"Well, first, you didn't lose your job. They took it away from you. Second, the world has not ended. Third, you have a career and a degree and a designation. Fourth, you are smart, and fifth, the world needs accountants everywhere. And last, you will be okay."

"You are sure."

"I am sure. Charlotte, nobody was as smart as you in school. You graduated top of the class in university too. Smart people always have jobs. But …"

"But what?"

"But you hopped into that firm as soon as you graduated, no looking around, no travel. You just went to work. Perhaps this is the time for you to see the world a bit. Did you get a package?"

Charlotte shared the terms of the agreement.

"No issue with paying the rent then."

"I also have some savings."

"Really? Look at you. Does Irene know?"

"No." Charlotte and Janine both knew that Irene would claim Charlotte's saved money if she knew about it.

"I think you need to have a plan before you tell your mother about the job so that she doesn't do the planning for you. Why don't you go online, find a travel group? Go away for a while. Go to Europe for a month, buy a train pass and just do what feels good."

"I can't do that."

"Why not? I would. You have no dependents and enough money saved to pay rent and anything else. Besides, a change from Beckerville and life with your mother would be better than jumping into another job right away. Go, Charlotte. Try something different."

Charlotte was born in Beckerville and had lived most of her life on a farm about twenty miles out of town. Her dad raised cattle, and they grew hay for winter feed. Life on the farm was close to nature and wide, open spaces. Charlotte loved it despite all the work required to grow a garden, keep a house, and manage a farm. She was an only child and helped both her parents. She preferred helping her dad. It was easier. Until he got sick.

She was in university then, just finished her last year, contemplating what was next. During that year, it was apparent her dad couldn't run the farm any longer and in a move that seemed rash to Charlotte, her parents sold the farm and relocated into town. Her dad asked her to return to Beckerville and look for work so she could her help mother look after him. Charlotte always thought Beckerville was a good town to grow up in, but never really gave much thought about living there all her life. The decision was made for her. The only good thing was that Janine was still there.

Janine's family moved almost every year since grade one. She had shared with Charlotte her experiences living in other places. Janine moved to Beckerville in grade seven and said it was an okay place, but her favorite was Calgary because she could see the mountains from their yard and the winters were warmer than anywhere else they had lived. Janine always thought she would return to Calgary, but Charlotte was glad she hadn't. Today she really needed her to be in Beckerville.

Charlotte looked at Janine and tried to imagine being in Europe on a train, arriving in London and walking along the Mall. Seeing the Louvre and the Mona Lisa in Paris. These were all things she had only ever seen online. Her eyes glittered and gleamed. Janine was right. It was time she did something for herself. Then a pull of responsibility dragged her back to reality.

"I'm not sure I should." Charlotte felt Janine's stare.

"Why don't you go home and think about it? It is a big step, but the opportunity is certainly now," Janine said.

Charlotte's shoulders sagged in relief. She wasn't ready

for such a big step. After all, she had been fired only a couple of hours ago. Surely that was enough change for one day?

"I think I better look for a new job."

Janine gasped, "Don't forget what I said."

"I won't. You are right. This is a time when I could go away. But I promised my dad."

They hugged, and Charlotte felt Janine's eyes on her as she waved goodbye from her Toyota. She wasn't sure if she was going to disappoint her friend if she didn't buy a plane ticket, but she felt like she just might. She tried shrugging that feeling off as she drove away, but she could feel it linger.

three

. . .

CHARLOTTE PARKED and walked quietly past Peewee who was asleep. She continued halfway down the block to the mailboxes and brought the mail back to the door of the house. She unlocked it and stood on the landing, glancing at the mail, but not paying attention. Her thoughts were on the morning. She looked up the three steps that led to her mother's half of the house and noted the shut door. There didn't seem to be any noise from the other side. Her mother wasn't home, or Charlotte would have heard the radio.

She turned to her left and opened the door to her suite, closing it behind her as she stepped down the stairs to the basement suite. They had added this suite for the nurse who cared for her dad full-time before he was moved to a long-term care facility. The basement suite had an open floor plan so that Charlotte could watch the TV from the kitchen as she cooked. Her bedroom was in a corner of the suite and the bathroom was tucked under the stairway—it held a generous sized shower. The windows let in some light, but not enough, and Charlotte felt the weight of the house above her, made more ominous by her mother's presence.

Charlotte promised her father that she would look after

her mother when he went into long-term care. The rent Charlotte paid covered Irene's expenses, including their utilities. The house was mortgage free, but her parents' investments were used up by the expense of a live-in nurse and then the long-term care facility. Many times, since her dad's passing, Charlotte had suggested that her mother should get a job, but Irene wasn't motivated. She claimed she was in mourning and needed time. It was six years since Charlotte's dad had passed away.

Charlotte's mind returned to the mail, but she just put it on the table without looking at it. At the little desk she had built into a closet, Charlotte powered up her computer and started scrolling through group trips and locations. Soon she got lost and didn't hear her mother open the door.

"You're home early." Irene startled Charlotte out of her exploration.

"Oh yeah. I am. Would you please knock?"

"Why?"

"It's the polite thing to do when coming into someone's home."

"But you are my daughter."

"It's just a knock."

"So why are you home?"

Charlotte turned in her chair and looked at her mother, mustering up the courage to admit what had happened. She didn't have to.

"You didn't get fired? I knew you would eventually. You can't be good at your job, or did you get caught having a fling with the boss?"

Charlotte's bottom jaw dropped. Wherever did that come from?

"No mother, I didn't get caught having an affair with the boss. I wouldn't do that."

"Well, obviously he wouldn't want you. You are too plain."

Charlotte stared at her mother, remembering what Janine always said about the crazies. "I got let go today, Mother."

"Let go. What does that mean?"

"That means I no longer have a job. They closed my department."

"Well, you obviously weren't good enough to keep. You'll just have to go out and find another job. Starting now. Is that what you are doing on that computer?" Irene craned her neck to see the screen. But Charlotte had clicked it off when her mother started speaking.

"How are you going to pay rent and utilities? You know I rely on your payments."

"I have enough until I find another job."

"Did they pay you to leave? They did not like you, did they? Figures. How much did you get?"

"None of your …"

"I'm your mother and you will tell me how much you got."

"I have enough to pay for the things I usually pay."

"Well, if you are one minute late, a good landlord would evict you."

"You wouldn't evict your daughter, would you? Especially after she just got let go from her job." Charlotte couldn't believe Irene could be that cruel.

"Well, no, but you need to find a job. I'll go upstairs and start looking for you." With that, Irene evaporated up the steps.

Charlotte remembered there was mail on the table but discovered it was all flyers and advertising, the kinds of thing put in everyone's mailbox hoping someone would bite. She noticed one piece that promoted a riverboat cruise in Europe and opened it. She looked at the beautiful vista, the calm waters, and the gorgeous plates of food. It was worth considering, at least for Janine. She threw the rest of the mail in the recycling.

four

. . .

THOUGH SHE TRIED, her heart wasn't into looking for work through the various job sites the next morning. She turned off her computer and grabbed her sweater. Perhaps a walk would help. She scanned out the window for Peewee before she opened the door. Today, she was lucky. She saw him asleep by his doghouse and quietly opened her door. She was about to step off the landing to the sidewalk when her mother's door opened, and Irene demanded to know where she was going. This noise woke up Peewee. He barked as loudly as Irene. Charlotte looked at them both and walked to the front of the house. Why would she want to stay around this?

Charlotte loved the tree-lined streets, the various parks scattered throughout, and the friendliness of the people in Beckerville. It was her hometown, and she hadn't thought much about leaving, especially after her dad passed away. With a university degree and her designation, she could make a life for herself somewhere else, just like Aunt Alice. Charlotte wondered why she suddenly remembered Aunt Alice. Her aunt had visited every summer since as early as Charlotte could remember. And then she suddenly stopped when Charlotte was about eight. That was twenty years ago.

Aunt Alice had made life in Victoria sound like a place Charlotte would want to visit. Aunt Alice told Charlotte how she left Beckerville to study at a university in Edmonton and be an independent woman.

"I was one of only a few women in my class. I worked hard for good marks, so it guaranteed me a good job. Working hard and smart is very important, Charlotte," she said. "Do you know the difference?"

"I think so."

And then, after some thought, Charlotte said, "Well, maybe not."

"Do the right things at the right time in the right way. Read a lot about everything. Get enough sleep, eat well, and move."

Charlotte changed everything after that. She liked ideas like that. Her mother's only ideas were how to make light buns and smooth gravy, ideas Charlotte wasn't much interested in. She didn't see them making her life great, and that's what Charlotte desired most, a great life. So far, until she moved back to Beckerville and got fired, she had done everything she could to create that great life.

She excelled in school and finished top of her class every year in high school. Though her mother didn't remark on it. Not an *Excellent work, Charlotte*. Not even *Congratulations..* It made Charlotte feel doing well in school wasn't important. But she did anyway. She wanted to go to university. To be like Aunt Alice.

Going to university had meant leaving Beckerville for a purpose and she had thought about staying in the big city after graduation, but her dad's illness had called her home. Her dad was everything her mother was not—kind in a word, thoughtful in deed, quiet in demeanor, and honorable in intention. Charlotte's eyes teared as she remembered hugs, jokes, card games, and looking at the stars with him. She continued her walk down the street.

Why was he the one who had to go first? Her hands flew to her mouth to recapture the words. She shook her head to shift her thoughts as she arrived at her favorite park. She hopped on the swing and swooped back and forth. As she flew, she remembered an earlier swing in the backyard on the farm.

Charlotte had made buns for the first time. She was twelve. They didn't work out. They had no round domes and were heavy, not light like her mother's.

"Oh, Charlotte. Your buns are no good. You'll never be a baker." Irene's observation cut Charlotte deep. "Maybe you'll have better luck with pies."

Charlotte's face had burned with shame as she ran outside to the swing. She seated herself on her favorite of the two seats—the highest. She pumped and pumped until she soared through the air. It rushed past her ears and the landscape moved up and down in front of her eyes. She watched the sky as the tears ran down her face. It seemed she would never do a thing that pleased her mother. *Was there anything she would be good at?*

Different tears for a different reason fell from her eyes as she finished swinging at the park. She wiped her face and returned home. The sadness spent. She managed to open her door unnoticed by both Irene and Peewee. She looked at the riverboat cruise flyer again and thought, *maybe.* A ding on her phone announced a text. It was an invitation for supper from her mother.

Why does she show up unannounced sometimes, and then text me other times? Charlotte was reminded of Janine's definition of crazies. It made her laugh as she climbed the stairs.

"We'll have to economize until you get a new job so I can only feed you soup and a sandwich," declared Irene as she ladled soup into Charlotte's bowl.

Grilled cheese sandwiches and cut vegetables were

already on the table when Charlotte sat down. Not sure if she wanted to ask the forbidden question, Charlotte did anyway, "Did you ever think of getting a job, Mother?"

"Why? Aren't you going to be able to get a job?"

"I'm sure I will. But it might be good for you to get out."

"I get out. I shop, I go to the library and I'm thinking about helping at the long-term care facility. They are looking for volunteers." Irene paused and looked up from ladling soup into her own bowl. "Why? Should I get out more?"

"You are too dependent on me; you need to depend on yourself."

"But you promised your father." Irene lifted her spoon to her mouth.

"I did, but I'm not sure he meant for the rest of my life."

The spoon clattered into the bowl, splashing soup on the table.

"Charlotte Irene Martin, you made a promise to your father. Don't you think helping me out is the least you can do? You are being very ungrateful after all we have done for you. Besides, I have never had a job. I don't have any skills. And I am too old."

"You are not too old Mother."

"Charlotte, when you are my age, you are invisible. How can I get a job when no one will even acknowledge me? You are going to have to support me for the rest of my life. That is what your father expected, and you will bloody well do that."

Charlotte decided she wasn't hungry and stood up from the table.

"Where are you going?"

"Home Mother." And she quietly left her mother's suite and descended into the space that was beginning to feel like a jail cell.

five

. . .

"I SPENT an hour this morning going over positions and applied for four of them." Charlotte shared over tea at Janine's the next afternoon.

"Good for you. Do they look like good ones?"

"Most of them were entry level accounting jobs."

"But you have experience and you graduated top of class. Doesn't that mean you should apply for something a little higher than entry level?"

Charlotte looked at Janine.

"Charlotte, you sell yourself short. I don't care what Old Fuzziewig said or did to you, you are a find, and many companies would be proud to have you on their staff. Set your sights a little higher."

"But those jobs are harder to find. What if I'm not good enough for what they want?"

"You are good enough and then some." And after a pause to sip her tea, "By the way, what happened with the travel idea?"

"Not much. I did see a flyer for European cruises on a riverboat."

"And ..."

"And it's on my table."

"But you are applying for jobs."

"I am still thinking about it."

"But you applied for four positions. That's not thinking about it."

Charlotte looked down at her teacup and then up at her friend with tears in her eyes. "Busted."

"Oh, Charlotte, what happened? What did Irene do now?"

Charlotte told her about their conversation over the interrupted meal the night before.

"Oh, she's scared."

"Scared? Of what?"

"Change. Of looking for a job. Of doing something different from anything she has ever done before."

"No, she's not. She wants me to honor what I told Dad I would do."

"Maybe, but I think it is more about what she has to do for herself. She is making a lot of noise around what you should do, but really it's about how scared she is. She won't be the boss at a job. She can't bully people. She will have to learn and be told what to do. She's never done that."

Charlotte considered what Janine said. "I am pulling my weight, like I promised Dad I would."

"And so …"

"I deserve a bit of a break, don't I?"

"Do you?"

"Yes. I do. I'm going home to look at that brochure again. Seriously, this time. Thanks, Janine. You are a girl's best friend."

"Well, don't leave without telling me where you are going and don't let Irene dissuade you from anything you plan. Promise?"

"Promise."

"I'll hold you to that."

They hugged. Charlotte got into her car, renewed with

energy and a surprising feeling of potential freedom. Janine was right. She had never been anywhere, and it was time. A month away would be fantastic. She could hardly wait to get home and start planning.

Charlotte parked her car in her spot at the back of the house. As she made her way to her doorstep, she walked by the fence, she gave Peewee a hard stare. He stared back at her and opened his mouth to bark. And then didn't. She watched him turn, walk to his doghouse, curl into a circle, and lay down.

Wow, she thought, collecting mail from the mailbox. She returned to the house and took the stairs down to her suite.

Her mother followed right behind her. Irene was relentless.

"How's the job hunt going?"

"Slow, but I applied for four jobs this morning." Charlotte placed the mail on the table.

"Good. You'll have to do that every day. I hear the job market is tight." Irene reached for the mail. "What's this?" Irene held out one of the letters from the table.

"I'm not sure, Mother. I didn't look at the mail."

"Well, you have a letter from someone in Victoria. Who do you know in Victoria?"

"No one."

"Well then, I should open it."

Charlotte grabbed the letter out of her mother's hand.

"It's addressed to me. I'll open it. Now if you don't mind, I have a job to look for." She was grateful for the diversion.

"You make sure you get another job. Right now." Irene stomped up the stairs and slammed Charlotte's door, then her own.

Charlotte took a deep breath. The severance money was not enough to find another place to live, but as soon as she got a job she was going to move. Even if it meant living in a studio unit or sharing an apartment with others. Enough of this.

She had promised Janine she would take a trip. She sighed. How would she manage it all? Find a new job. Get a new place to live. Escape her mother. And travel. That seemed like a lot in a short time. Should she really make all those changes? Was her life here really that bad? She shook her head. She wasn't like Janine, who had found a good man, married him, had two kids, and loved being home. Janine worked from her house designing and selling knitting patterns online. She got to be creative and at home and contribute to their finances. She had managed to find a balance between self-fulfillment and being a mom.

Charlotte envied that seeming simplicity. She thought her life would always be complicated by having to look after Irene. Charlotte suspected Irene could look after herself, especially if she got a job, but Irene was clear she wasn't ready to work. Charlotte was sensitive to her mother's grieving. Charlotte felt stuck. The dream she had of a great life of challenging work, a pleasant home, and some travel, seemed to have moved out of her reach.

Charlotte stared at herself in the mirror over the couch. It was made of six rectangles, each beveled on all four edges. The rectangles hung side by side and provided a slightly skewed reflection. It originally belonged to her grandparents and had hung over their couch. Charlotte remembered making faces in it as a child because it could distort her face and made her laugh. She now saw slices of her reflection and thought, *That's pretty much how I feel—split into multiple personalities, not one of them the true, happy me. This is your chance, Charlotte. You can change everything and find a life out there. A life that you really love.*

With tea steeping in a pot and a mug before her, Charlotte sat at her table and looked at the letter her mother had grabbed from her. She turned the envelope over, looking for clues to its contents as the tea steeped to her preferred slightly black color. Using a knife, she slit open the letter and read its first lines.

Dear Charlotte. I am your Aunt Alice. Your mother's sister. You probably don't remember me. I thought it was time we reconnected.

Charlotte pushed her chair back.

six

· · ·

CHARLOTTE PICKED up the letter again but didn't finish reading it. She pondered remembrances of Aunt Alice. They were vague, like an old TV show she had watched as a child. Aunt Alice lived on Vancouver Island, but Charlotte had only seen it on a map. She remembered regular summer visits her aunt made to Beckerville until she was eight. They had conversation about life, school, and friends. They'd spent time exploring the farm and swimming at the lake. She remembered hugs and kisses on the cheek, holding hands, running, and laughing. Aunt Alice was a welcome diversion in the summer. She remembered a conversation with her mother on the summer of her ninth birthday.

"Mother, is Aunt Alice coming this summer?"

"No."

"Why not?"

"I don't know. She wouldn't say. She just said she wasn't coming this summer or ever again."

"No reason?"

"Nope."

Charlotte considered their time together. It was everything lovely, fun, and joyous—not like life was at home. She couldn't imagine what she might have done to turn her aunt away.

"Maybe I should talk to her?"

"No." Her mother's voice was as sharp as fall sleet.

Charlotte felt the frost but ventured on. "Why not?"

The storm that was her mother let loose. "Why is she so important to you? She doesn't live here. She doesn't take care of you. She comes and goes as she wishes; she lives the life of a free, single woman. God knows what she gets up to. She says all she does is work."

Charlotte remembered her mother turning to face and her, eyes narrowed like that of the black cat that lived down the street. "I saw you two together, holding hands, and laughing. Talking like you had secrets I shouldn't hear. What is it you two talked about?"

Her mother hadn't cared about her conversations with Aunt Alice when she visited. Suddenly, it seemed like they were vitally important to her.

"Nothing." Charlotte would not reveal she could open her heart with Aunt Alice and talk about everything and anything. Aunt Alice listened, asked questions, but never told her what to do. She couldn't tell her mother that she wasn't easy to talk to. Irene was so judgmental.

"You must have said or done something because she isn't coming back. We are not talking about it again."

Charlotte thought about writing to her aunt after that, to find out what really happened. She feared her mother would find out, so she didn't. She pushed Aunt Alice deep into her memories, distant but not forgotten. Now, Aunt Alice wanted to open that door.

I am sorry we have lost touch. I thought it was time we knew each other. You must have a job by now. I wondered if you had some holiday time coming up soon. I am running an animal rescue center and need some help for a couple of weeks. You could stay with me if you are comfortable with that. We could spend time together, like we did when I used to visit.

Could you at least think about coming? Please invite your mother as well. I have asked her to come before, but she has never accepted. Maybe she will if you ask her. No obligation.

Your Aunt Alice.

Alice had signed her name with a flourish on the A and she had provided her email address.

Charlotte considered the invitation. She should look for a job, but she had enough money to manage for a few months. Finding a job wasn't urgent, despite what her mother said. Charlotte had never been to Vancouver Island. It would be a pleasant break. A change of scenery. Not a train ride in Europe, but a change. While she pondered, she heard the door open and saw her mother standing on the top step.

Charlotte never admitted it to anyone, but her mother reminded her of Maleficent, the wicked witch of *Sleeping Beauty*. Irene wore long flowing caftans, often in black and purple. She swirled into a room when she entered, preceded by a blast of cold air. Her hair was not black like Maleficent's but its grey was as daunting. Her dark brown eyes added to the overall sinister image. Charlotte hid her smile as she looked at Irene in the doorway. It was funny, scary, and absurd.

"Is that a letter from my sister?" Irene's eyes slitted.

"Yes. How did you know?"

"Because you don't know anybody. The only person we know in Victoria is my sister Alice. What does she want?"

"Why would she want anything?"

"We haven't heard from her in over twenty years. Why else would she write? Maybe she has finally fallen on her face, like Momma always said she would, and she needs our help. She is going to have to beg if she wants my help. Give me that letter, let me read it." Irene ripped it from Charlotte's hand before she could hide it behind her. Irene stilled as she read it. "She wants you to come to see her and reconnect. Isn't that nice?" Except Irene's voice didn't make it sound pleasant at all. Her sarcasm made it seem an unreasonable request.

"She invited you too."

"Oh, I'll not be going. I've ignored her other letters. Why would that change now? She needs something from us, not a family reunion."

"Why would you ignore an invitation from your sister?"

"Because she's out of my life."

"Well, I'm going. I've missed her visits. It would be good to reconnect."

"You have no job and no money, your rent is due on Friday, and utilities are due next week. You can't possibly go. I won't allow you to live here for free."

"I don't expect to live for free. I have enough money to pay for what needs paying while I am gone, plus whatever else you think I owe you."

"Oh, you could never afford to pay me for what you owe me."

"What do you mean?"

Irene looked like she had inadvertently let out a secret.

"Mother, what do you mean I couldn't afford to pay you what I owe you?"

"Oh, every parent thinks their child owes them. For what they provided, the home, food, and clothes."

"Isn't that what a parent does?"

"It is. Just sometimes I don't think you appreciate what I sacrificed for you."

"What you and Dad sacrificed for me."

"Of course. It isn't just about me, is it? Anyway, you can't go. You need to find a job. I found a bunch on the internet for you to apply for. I sent you an email with the links."

Charlotte took a deep breath. She seemed to always be

doing deep breathing exercises around her mother. Spending the next few weeks at home receiving her mother's chosen selection of job opportunities and being checked on didn't appeal to her. Applying for a passport and booking travel to Europe would take weeks. Visiting a stranger, well almost a stranger, a few hundred kilometers away seemed like a great idea. She opened the drawer under her computer desk and pulled out a checkbook.

"Mother, I am writing you a check for two months' rent and utilities. Then I am going to book a flight to Victoria."

"You can't possibly have enough money to pay me all that now."

"I do. Now if you will leave me alone, I need to get some things done." Charlotte stood as tall as she could and moved toward her mother.

Irene's eyes opened wide and then closed. She stomped to the door. "Don't you listen to anything Alice has to say about me. It is all lies."

Puzzled, Charlotte stood at the bottom of the steps.

"Mother, what could Aunt Alice possibly tell me I don't already know about you?" She shut the door behind her mother and this time locked it. She wanted no more interruptions.

seven

. . .

CHARLOTTE STOOD GAZING into her closet. What to pack for a trip to a place you've never been to? She stood with her arms crossed and one hand on her cheek as she gazed at her wardrobe, trying to decide.

She bought her plane ticket online that morning for a flight the next day. Fast, she knew. Another opportunity to escape might not come. Janine's voice from their phone conversation that morning whispered to her.

"Charlotte, go. This is a sign. You don't need Europe; you've got Vancouver Island handed to you. Besides, your aunt will put you up, so your expenses won't be so much. If that is what you are worried about. That is what you are worried about, right?"

"Well, sort of, but actually, I don't know Aunt Alice very well. She used to come visit when I was younger and then she just stopped. It has been a long time."

"But they are wonderful memories."

"Oh, yeah. We used to explore the pond and the woods. She was one of a few adults who talked to me like I was a person. Like I had an opinion. That what I wanted mattered."

"You know people don't change. Unless something nasty

happens to them. Your aunt will be lovely. In fact, I bet you will want to stay there."

———

Charlotte pondered that as she stared at her clothes. Not really seeing them. She wondered if she could leave Beckerville. It was her hometown. All she knew. But what had kept her here? Surely not just her mother, or her promise to her father?

She frowned when there was a knock on her door. As Charlotte unlocked it Irene burst in. Charlotte stood still and let her mother finish her inspection, having endured this scrutiny many times while she had lived in the basement.

"What are you doing?"

"I'm deciding what I am going to pack."

"What are you packing for?"

"I am going to Victoria, remember Aunt Alice's invitation?"

"I do, but I thought you would come to your senses and change your mind. Why ever would you go?"

"Well, first because she invited me. Second, because I don't have a job. And a brief holiday would be ideal."

"She is just being nice. She wasn't serious about you coming to visit. She only suggested it, she didn't really invite you."

"Why would she just be nice? Why wouldn't she be serious?"

"I don't know. She's just that way. When you get there, she will ignore you while she is busy chasing her work. She will leave you to your own devices all the time. Is that what you want? To be alone in a place you don't know?"

"It won't be that way."

"Well, I think it will. Besides, you need to get a job. You

can't just go gallivanting off being unemployed. The neighbors will think I raised a leech on society."

"Mother, I have never been a leech on anyone. I paid my way through university. And I doubt the neighbors ever think about me."

"Well, you have your father to thank for that. If he hadn't saved so much, you wouldn't be debt-free, and I would be in a far better financial position."

"Mother, you know that isn't true. There is no mortgage. You only need money for groceries and utilities. Why don't you get a job? It's time, Dad's been gone for six years now."

"I'm too old to find work. Who is going to hire me? Besides, you promised your father you would look after me. And right now, I can't count on rent money if you are unemployed. Really Charlotte, you can be so inconsiderate of me and my needs. It is so irresponsible of you."

"Mother, I have been responsible since the day I was born."

"Your father and I instilled that sense of responsibility in you."

Charlotte was tired of this sparring. It was a broken record that played over and over between them. She wished she was flying out that afternoon.

"What did you really want Mother?"

"Oh, I wondered if you had some sugar I could borrow. I'm out."

Charlotte filled a small container and handed it to her mother.

"I warn you; you'll be there alone. Running a business means no time for anything else." Irene swirled and vanished, slamming the door behind her.

Charlotte sat, letting an exhausted whoosh escape from her mouth. Irene was more daunting than usual today. She thought about what her mother said about Aunt Alice. She retrieved the letter from her desk and re-read it. There was nothing indicating Aunt Alice wouldn't spend time with her. In fact, her aunt's words were very welcoming. *It's time we got to know each other.* That sounded like an invitation. She got up and threw the letter on the desk. Time to get back to the closet and what to pack. Charlotte decided her back-up plan would be to pick up a Vancouver Island travel book at the airport. That would help her explore on her own should her mother's prophecy turned out to be true.

eight

. . .

AS JANINE DROVE Charlotte to the airport early the next morning, Charlotte needed reassurance.

"Should I have ignored the letter and booked a flight to Europe?" Charlotte asked.

"And miss a chance to know another family member? Perhaps a pleasant one? No way. This is the right thing to do."

"I feel that too. But it makes me nauseous at the same time."

"Why?"

"Mother thought I should stay and find a job. She threatened to evict me if I didn't get one. She is afraid I won't pay her rent."

"Your mother is a big bully. What did you tell her?"

"I gave her two months' rent and paid the utilities just to make her go away."

"That was probably wise. What did she say about her sister?"

"That she was a self-serving, professional with no time for a family and therefore, morally lacking."

"Wow. What did Alice ever do to her?"

"I don't know. Whatever it was, it was big."

"Maybe you will find out in Victoria?"

"Maybe. I'm not sure I care. I am more interested in getting to know Aunt Alice. It would be lovely to have a family member I like."

"Charlotte, I have never heard you say you don't like your mother."

"It seems wrong to say that about a parent. About someone who gave birth to you and raised you. It sounds ungrateful."

"She isn't a likeable person."

"I know."

"How did you turn out so good?"

"My dad."

"True, he made you able to handle all that she has dealt out without losing your mind. Although I have always felt you knew deep down, there was a better way to live."

"There has to be. I just haven't quite found it yet. In fact, I almost quit believing it until I thought I was in line for a promotion. I figured it would change everything. That plan got foiled."

"Maybe this is the real plan."

"Maybe."

They hugged at the departures drop off.

"Keep in touch."

———

Charlotte watched the mountains and meadows roll by far below her plane window. She wondered again if she was doing the right thing. She opened the travel book and turned some pages. It occurred to her if she didn't want to stay in Victoria, she could just fly back home. Return to the safety of home with what she knew. Didn't like but knew.

The book revealed lots of intriguing places to explore. She

could see them on her own if need be. For now, she would give her aunt the benefit of the doubt and get to know her, like she'd asked. After all, her memories were of a kind woman who made her feel like she was very important. Aunt Alice couldn't have changed that much.

———

Aunt Alice was only a little taller than Charlotte now. She remembered her being much taller, but then Charlotte had been eight when they last met. Aunt Alice's shoulder length hair was in the same loose style she wore back then, but there was a little grey along the sides. She still smelled of the same perfume. It reminded Charlotte of roses and lilies.

"Charlotte."

Charlotte sank into a hug that felt like warm hot chocolate and wool socks on a winter day.

"Aunt Alice."

"Charlotte. Your face hasn't changed since I last saw you. You're taller, but you still have that same serene face and beautiful golden hair."

"I was a young girl, then. It was a long time ago."

"It must be over twenty years ago."

"A long time. Why did you stop coming?"

Aunt Alice paused and looked at Charlotte and then took her arm to move them to the baggage carousel. "Let's talk about that at home. I am so glad you came."

"I am too."

The sky was clear of clouds and cerulean blue. The ocean's salty breeze permeated the car as they drove into the city.

"This is beautiful."

"I know. I have loved it here since the first day I came."

"When was that?"

Aunt Alice spent the rest of the drive reminding Charlotte how she ended up in Victoria. "After university, I worked for an accounting firm in Beckerville. When an opportunity came up to move to the island, I applied and was chosen. I have loved it here ever since."

"Are you still an accountant?"

"Not really. A few years back, I decided I needed a work change; fewer hours, more freedom. I searched but found nothing in my profession. I had been volunteering at the rescue center, for years, walking dogs. The executive director mentioned they were looking for an accountant. It was exactly right for me. The hours I wanted and more time with the dogs."

"Did you miss the work? It was quite a step down."

"Oh, I was not interested in a busy office any longer. It was time for me to let go."

"Was it hard to leave everything you knew and were comfortable with?"

"It was, but I was ready." Charlotte heard confidence in her aunt's voice.

They reached the parking lot of a three-story building.

"We'll go there tomorrow, and you can look around, meet the animals and the staff. Today, let's get you settled and just visit."

The apartment layout was like nothing Charlotte had ever seen, and she was in love immediately. The center of the apartment started with a utility room beside the entrance door, then a kitchen that flowed into a dining area, then to the living room. You could see the mountains and ocean from as far back as the kitchen counter.

The spare bedroom was bigger than Charlotte's at home. Five pillows were piled on the double bed covered by a duvet that seemed to float on it. A small writing desk was next to the bed, and the closet had hangers waiting for Charlotte's clothes. A doorway led to an ensuite bathroom with a shower. *Nice.* On the other side of the bed sliding doors opened to a deck. The deck stretched across the width of the apartment.

There were doors from the deck to the living room that Charlotte had seen when she entered the apartment. *That third set of doors at the far end must be to Aunt Alice's room*, Charlotte thought.

Back in the center of the apartment Charlotte walked to the deck. Before her lay a stretch of water, colored in a mix of grey and blue. Across the water was a range of mountains topped with a sprinkle of snow. The day was warm, the wind was soft. She closed her eyes and listened to the chirp of birds and the waves hitting the beach. All new to Charlotte. So different from Beckerville. She felt her heart swell up and knew she had made the right choice to come.

"Lovely, isn't it?"

"Oh, Aunt Alice. I understand why you stayed here. This is amazing. Beckerville has nothing like this at all."

"I know, I have never regretted spending my life here. I missed my parents, especially my dad, but I felt this is where I belonged."

Charlotte looked at her aunt. She wanted to ask what it was like to belong somewhere but didn't want to reveal her own insecurities so soon. Time enough for that once she knew she could trust her aunt again.

"Come back in, let's have a bite to eat. Do you like ham and cheese?"

"Of course. Let me help."

They took the Black Forest ham and Havarti cheese sandwiches on soft buns to the small table on the deck and sat in the sun's warmth eating and chatting. Aunt Alice pointed out the geography. "Those mountains are the Olympic Mountains of Washington state and this body of water is the Strait of Juan de Fuca. It stretches over to Vancouver and down to Seattle, where it becomes the Puget Sound. That way stretches to the Pacific Ocean. When we have finished lunch, why don't we walk on the beach? Unless you are too tired?"

"No, I'm good. I would love a walk."

There was a paved beach pathway between the street and the water that seemed to run on forever. They started off toward a rocky point that Aunt Alice called Clover Point.

"I walk the path between Clover Point and the breakwater every day. It keeps me moving and clears my head."

Charlotte inhaled the air and let the sun's heat warm her whole body. The tension of the past days eased and floated away in the wind. Her aunt was easy to be with.

"You are smiling."

"This is good. I forgot what it is like to just be. I feel like I am getting medicine just by walking."

"That's an excellent description. Walking and nature is good for anything that is ailing you. You must have a busy job."

"Had."

"Had?"

Charlotte felt embarrassed to admit what had happened but felt safe sharing. "I got let go this week. They were eliminating departments and said I was redundant."

Aunt Alice stopped and held Charlotte by her shoulders, taking in the face of her niece.

Charlotte looked into sympathetic eyes that comforted her.

"Oh my, that's a blow. How are you doing?"

"Oh, it devastated me at first because I'd thought I was in line for a promotion. My friend Janine said I should take a break and travel for a month. I was looking at trips to Europe when your letter came."

"And here you are."

"This seemed like a good idea."

"Well, I am very glad you accepted my invitation. I promise it will not be boring and I promise we will have lots of walks and lots of conversations."

Aunt Alice paused, as if considering whether to say the next sentence. "How is your mother?"

"Mother? Oh, the usual. Grumpy, unhappy, lonely. She wasn't crazy about me coming here."

"What did she say?"

Charlotte wasn't sure how to answer but decided being truthful wouldn't be wrong. "That you were—"

"I need to sit. Let's stop here." Aunt Alice sat down on a bench along the path. She seemed to catch her breath and then offered, "You can tell me, I'm sure I have heard it before."

Charlotte wasn't sure if her aunt was out of breath or usually sat her during her walk. The spot was so perfect she assumed the latter.

"Mother wondered what you wanted. She thinks you want help from us. She didn't want me to come, said that I should not listen to anything you have to say about her, and that she definitely wasn't coming."

"All that, eh?"

"Oh, and more. She said she had ignored your earlier letters and your invitations. You wrote before?"

"I did."

"How come I didn't know?"

"Ask your mother that question."

Charlotte turned to look at her aunt. "Why did you write?"

"To keep in touch."

"I'm glad you tried."

"Me too."

"Sorry you had to wait so long to see me."

Aunt Alice put her arm around Charlotte and gave her another warm hug. Charlotte couldn't remember two hugs in one day, ever. And they were such lovely hugs. She wanted to hold on to her aunt. She could feel that she was on the brink of having all her stresses and sadness cascade away over a waterfall if she just held onto this hug a little longer. But she held back. Not yet. Not on the first day.

Charlotte turned her head to hide her tears when Aunt Alice released her.

"Charlotte, are you okay?"

"I am. Give me a minute."

"Irene is that bad?"

"She's hard to be with."

"She wasn't always that way. She used to be fun and happy, but something happened, and she was never the same."

"What?"

"Momma made her do something. Gave her no choice. And I think it was more than Irene could handle, but she wasn't going to say no to Momma."

"What was it?"

"Oh, time enough for that later. That's a serious conversation for scotch on the deck." She rose, kept an arm around Charlotte and led them toward the Ogden Point Breakwater.

Charlotte settled into the warmth of the day and of her companion.

"So, what are you going to do about the job?"

"Look for one when I get home. I'll get a good reference from my firm, and I am good at what I do. I will find another job."

"Good for you."

"And I am going to find my own place."

"You're still living with your mother?"

"I live in the basement suite they built when Dad was sick. I promised him I would look after Mother after he …"

"Your dad was a prince. I don't know how Irene got so lucky with him. He could handle her so well. Especially when she went into those dark places she hid in. I always wondered if he was happy."

"He seemed to be. He never complained. He had work he loved, and he was always in his shop making something out of wood. I miss him."

"I bet you do. But I think that your mother is probably doing better than you think. It's time she found a life for herself. Did she ever get a job?"

"No. She said Dad agreed she didn't have to work."

"Even after your dad passed?"

"I think she thought she would be okay. Especially when I moved into the basement suite. But I think it is a little too lonely, and she hasn't any friends. So, she relies on me—a lot." And after a breath. "I think she misses Dad. But she would never say. She doesn't talk about him at all." Charlotte looked down at her hands wrapped around each other.

"You've given her six years. That's a lot by anyone's standard. You could force her hand to get a job and just move. It won't break your promise to your dad. He wouldn't have expected you to stay forever."

"How do you know?"

"I know she's okay. I may not have been in touch for all these years, but Irene is stronger than she lets on. Looking after herself would likely be good for her."

"Aunt Alice, you make it all sound so easy."

"Well, I'm not sure it is easy. Choosing your own life isn't usually easy. But it is your right. Just like your mom chooses to be what she is, grumpy. It keeps people away."

"It does."

"She put up a wall and won't let people in and then is mad because no one comes in!" Aunt Alice said.

"You do know her well. Why did you stop coming to see us?"

"She asked me to."

nine

. . .

CHARLOTTE WASN'T sure she'd heard correctly.

"Mother told you to stay away. Why would she do that?"

"She said she didn't want me to get close to you."

"But why would she worry about that?"

"I think she thought you would love me more. Your mother worries about being good enough."

"Why?" Perhaps Aunt Alice could give some insight into her mother.

"When we were little, Irene and Momma, Gramma Beatrice to you, were very close. Momma had very exacting standards. I watched Irene bend over backwards to please Momma. Except Momma was never happy. We could never set the table property. We could never iron the clothes with as crisp edges as our mother did. We could never clean as well as she did. I gave up early, realizing I didn't care enough about those things. But it mattered to your mother. She needed Momma's approval. I think she felt it put her in first place in Momma's affections."

"Did you get into trouble for not doing things Gramma Beatrice's way?"

"Oh yeah. I was always in her bad books. Luckily our dad

needed help in the barn and the fields, and so I could go hide there. He was grateful for the company and the help. Life was so much easier with Dad."

"Sounds like Mother had it rough." Charlotte observed.

"She did, but she did it to herself. I was always asking her what she needed the approval for."

"What did she say?"

"She said that she needed to show that Momma was a good teacher, and that Irene was a good daughter."

"Well, she runs her house the same way Gramma Beatrice ran hers."

"You mean she was hard on you too?" Aunt Alice stopped walking.

"Yeah, but I was like you, I just didn't care. She was always mad at me. It was like I challenged her values."

"I think it was more like you ignored her importance."

Charlotte considered it. "Maybe."

"There are a lot of similarities between Beatrice Knight and Irene Martin. Stubborn attitudes, acrylic walls built around them, bullies, women without careers who were critical of those that did, buried in old value systems that don't hold any longer. Or at least weren't important to me. The apple didn't fall far from the tree."

"It is like we are oranges growing on apple trees." Charlotte observed.

"It is."

Charlotte looked at her aunt. Finally, there was someone else besides Janine and her father who understood what it was like to be Irene's daughter.

Aunt Alice enfolded Charlotte in a hug that made the tears well up in Charlotte's eyes. She didn't let them fall. She wasn't quite ready to show Aunt Alice how sad she really felt.

ten

. . .

CHARLOTTE SLOWLY STEPPED out of her aunt's car. She wasn't sure what to expect, so she was very watchful. There were no dogs in the immediate vicinity, or on the pathway to the door of the center's office, so she relaxed a little. She could hear barks and yips from the other side of the fence.

"Charlotte, are you okay?"

"First time, trying to figure out where to go." Charlotte would not tell her aunt what her genuine concern was. She didn't want Aunt Alice to be disappointed in her or to regret her decision to bring Charlotte to the center.

"This way then."

"You lead the way."

Charlotte followed her aunt into the center that was once a house. They entered the kitchen where three women were at the table with teacups in hand and cookies on a plate. Aunt Alice motioned for Charlotte to take an empty seat.

"Everyone, this is Charlotte." As she introduced her, she poured them both a cup of tea.

One by one, the others at the table introduced themselves.

The oldest one was Sandy, a small white-haired woman

with grey-blue eyes that smiled so warmly that Charlotte couldn't help but like her on sight. "Hello dearie. Your aunt has talked of nothing but your visit."

Next to Sandy sat Teresa, a taller, dark-haired lady with bright red lipstick. "Welcome to Victoria, Charlotte. Have you been here before?"

"Actually, no. This is my first time."

"Well, I'm sure your aunt is the best person to give you a tour of our island. She has talked of nothing else since you said you were coming. And we are so excited to meet you."

No one had ever said they were excited to see her. It was a good feeling.

The last person at the table was Bonnie. She had dark blonde hair tied into a ponytail and wore blue nail polish. "Welcome. How long are you here for?"

"Two weeks."

"Then back to your actual life."

"Then back to my actual life." Somehow that felt hollow, and Charlotte sank into silence. The prospect already depressed her.

The others started talking about the latest intake of dogs. Sandy provided the update. "We have two new dogs that came in this morning and there was a phone call about a stray just found off Blenkinsop. It's on its way."

Alice looked at the whiteboard on the wall that showed the layout of the center with the pens labelled with dog's names. "Where are we putting them?"

"The first two, Jango and Chutney, are going into pens nine and ten, but I'm not sure where we will put the stray yet. Perhaps in one of the run pens until we find a permanent home."

"Well Charlotte, it looks like we will put you to work right away. Would you rather walk a dog or help clean up pens?" Aunt Alice raised her eyebrows.

"Oh, um." Charlotte hadn't expected to be tasked with

dog chores, her aunt just mentioned that the accounting needed to be brought up to date. "I think cleaning pens." It seemed the safest.

"Come with me and I'll show you how we clean pens." Teresa stood up from the table, carrying her teacup and saucer to the sink. "Let's get our supplies and get you what you need." They walked to a shed in the yard. Teresa poked her head and arms into it and handed out a spray bottle, a pair of gloves, and two rags. "There, that should be it. I'll turn on the hose and show you what to do."

"Will any dogs be in the pens?" Charlotte felt the sweat on her forehead.

"Oh, no. Sandy will have moved them to the outside cages. It makes it easier when one person moves dogs and someone else does the cleaning."

The chore was relatively easy; pile up the toys and blankets outside the pens, pick up any dog waste, spray the spot with disinfectant, and rinse the cement floor. Let the floor dry and make up the bed with clean blankets and toys. Teresa left her to get the job done.

Charlotte felt totally competent. This she could handle. Then, she heard a car door slam, and someone yelled, "Hello, is anyone around?"

Charlotte peeked out of her pen and saw no one. She waited for someone to respond and when no one did she yelled back, "Hang on, I'll be right there." She walked to the gate that secured the yard to find a woman with her hand on the door of her car. At the window was a medium-sized dog, barking, and pawing at the window.

Charlotte stopped still. She needed to find someone. She turned, looking here and there, trying to figure out what to do. Footsteps came from behind and she spun on her heel, grateful to be rescued. She turned to return to her task.

"Hang on, Charlotte. This one will need a few hands." Teresa handed a leash and collar to Charlotte.

"But I can't ... I've never ...." she stammered.

"Come on, Charlotte. I'll tell you what to do."

Teresa opened the back passenger door, sat on the edge of the seat and turned to face the dog on the seat beside her. The dog was hunched against the door as far from Teresa as it could get. She talked calmly and held out her hand for the dog to sniff. She offered it a treat. The dog took it quickly. She patted the side of its head, still murmuring. Soon the dog was sitting on her lap, and it was eating the other treats she offered.

This might be easier than I expected, thought Charlotte.

"Charlotte, come around to the door and hand me that leash and collar, would you? Move slowly and quietly."

Teresa took the collar from her first. The dog snarled at Charlotte, who stepped back, surprised. She thought Teresa had the dog under control.

"Hang on, sweetie. We are here to help." Teresa almost cooed to the dog. "Now the leash, Charlotte."

Teresa clipped the leash to the collar and then turned to get out of the car with the dog still in her arms. She slowly lowered it to the ground, and the dog stood up and turned to Charlotte immediately snarling again.

"Charlotte, why don't you back away slowly, she obviously doesn't like your perfume." Teresa had a twinkle in her eye and then returned her attention to the dog. "Come on sweetie, let's find you a new home."

Charlotte stepped away. The dog easily followed Teresa away from the car, and Charlotte took a deep breath. Charlotte escorted the woman into the house.

Sandy motioned for the woman to take a seat at the kitchen table. "I'll take over from here Charlotte," said Sandy. "Finish up the pen you were cleaning and then I think your aunt is waiting for you in her office."

Charlotte breathed a sigh of relief but wondered if she could handle being at the center.

———

"How was that?" Charlotte felt Aunt Alice's eyes on her face as she leaned back in her chair.

"How was what?"

"I hear we have a new dog."

"Oh, it was okay. Teresa sure has a way with them. She must have a gift."

"No, just some knowledge and practice. Each dog is different, but we learn the same tactics so everyone can be competent. We'll train you on them this week. I think for now, it is time for you to help walk the dogs."

"I thought you wanted me to look at the accounts?" Charlotte felt the sweat on her forehead.

"The dogs need walking more. Come on."

As they walked to the dog pens, Charlotte looked around her. "How big is the property, Aunt Alice?"

"About fifteen acres. Why don't I give you a tour while we walk Cocoa?"

Cocoa hadn't been moved outside and lay on her blanket in her pen. She lifted her head and wagged her tail but stayed still when Aunt Alice opened the gate.

"Good morning, Cocoa. How are you today? Ready for a walk?" Aunt Alice bent to stroke Cocoa's head and body and then put the collar and leash on the dog. Cocoa happily followed Aunt Alice out of the pen and into the yard.

"Sit Cocoa," Aunt Alice commanded, and the dog sat. Aunt Alice reached into her pants pocket and pulled out a treat and offered it to Cocoa. Cocoa gently took the treat from her and gulped it down. She looked up in hopes of more.

"Cocoa is very calm and easy. You will enjoy walking her. She will take her cues from you. If you are calm, she will be too. Hold out your hand when you approach her, with the fist facing down, like this." Aunt Alice clenched her hand into a fist and turned it so the back of her hand faced up. "Let her sniff it. She may lick you or not. Once she seems used to your hand, then touch her, but move slowly and touch her on the side of the face. Some dogs feel that a hand over their head feels like a threat. Be slow and gentle with your movements. Talk softly to them and be friendly. Give it a try."

Charlotte approached Cocoa as her aunt instructed. It delighted her when Cocoa started licking. She softly stroked the dog's cheek.

"Do you want to walk her?" Aunt Alice offered the leash.

"Is it okay if you do it and I just watch this time?" Charlotte hoped her reluctance would be read as a lack of confidence instead of plain fear.

Aunt Alice offered Charlotte the leash. "She walks easily by your side, Charlotte. Give it a try. Now, where was I? Oh, right. This used to be a part of a grain farm and a bit of an orchard. We have converted the fields to garden for fresh produce that we sell at the farmer's markets. The fruit as well." Her arms waved out to the fence line that bordered along a plowed field. "We are just getting ready to plant the next rotation of vegetables. And the trees are just coming into bloom."

They walked a dirt path along the fence line which bordered the forest. The little poodle followed placidly along, not tugging on the leash, walking right beside Charlotte.

"She's great."

"Well trained," Aunt Alice said.

"How did she end up here?"

"Her owner was diagnosed with cancer and couldn't care for her any longer. I offered to take Cocoa."

"Will she get adopted even though she is older?"

"Oh, a retired gentleman has already adopted her. He is picking her up tomorrow. They are a perfect match."

The path led through the forest to a large body of water.

"This is the end of the property. There is a tiny house there, more of a shed really, a dock, and my sailboat."

"You sail?"

"I sail. I'll take you out while you are here."

Charlotte smiled. "I would like that. You sure have a full life here."

"Isn't that our job? Live a lot of life?"

Charlotte thought about that. "I never thought about it like that. I just thought you got a job and a desirable place to live."

"I think that works for many people. A long time ago I figured that there was more to life than work and a house. I intended to add as much to life as I could handle. That's how I ended up here. The farm was for sale and the dog rescue place I volunteered at was being forced to give up their home when a developer bought the property. So, I put two and two together, and figured it was time to stop being an accountant and be something else. Now I am a bookkeeper, groomer, walker, cleaner, and fundraiser for the center. It's so different, but I just love it."

"I can see why. The location is stunning, and the animals have a safe space here. They must be happy."

"I think they are. Some of them have had a very hard time and they aren't very trusting. Most of our work here is to regain their trust in humans, so that they can go back to living with a family."

"Do they all find homes?"

"You know, so far we have been lucky. We have found good homes for almost all of them."

"And when you don't?"

"Someone ends up with a new dog in the family. Sandy has a large acreage, and she has taken a few home with her, on a temporary basis and then ended up keeping them. She calls them foster fails. But I don't think she minds. Here's the dock."

A wooden dock jutted out into the bay, and a sailboat was tied to it. It bobbed up and down from front to back as the waves from a passing boat ran to shore. The water looked like a river that ran past the dock, and Aunt Alice pointed out to the curve explaining that the water fed into a bigger bay and then the ocean.

"I thought it was a bonus when I found this dock, and little shed on the property. I could have a sailboat and tie it up close, so I can go out easily any time."

Charlotte looked at the sailboat wondering what it would be like to know how to sail. "Have you sailed for a long time?"

"About thirty years now. I started with some friends at work, and we did all kinds of fooling around on boats. We did some trips around the island, one in the Caribbean and one in Europe. Now I sail into the bay and around this part of the island. That's enough adventure for me these days."

Charlotte shook her head. "There is so much I don't know about you, Aunt Alice."

"All the more reason for us to spend time together Charlotte," Aunt Alice gave Charlotte another hug.

"Come on. Let's get back to the center. It is probably time for us to pack up and go home. Are you hungry for supper? I have a salmon in the fridge for us."

They enjoyed supper on the deck in the warmth of the sun. Charlotte thought life was perfect in Victoria and was happy that her fear of dogs was still a secret.

eleven

· · ·

AFTER SUPPER, Aunt Alice grabbed a sweater from the hook by the door. "Come on, Charlotte. Time for a walk on the beach. I'll introduce you to the best ice cream in Canada." Charlotte donned a light sweater against the ever-present breeze, and they crossed the busy road to the beach pathway that ran along the coast.

"It's hard not to love this place." Charlotte couldn't help but compare it to the dry world inland that was fraught with winter and snow and cold.

"It was a pleasant change from Beckerville. It offered everything I wanted in life, an outdoor lifestyle without winter, fresh produce, challenging work, and once I found my apartment, I felt life was complete."

"Was it?"

"To some extent. I knew that there was a missing piece. Family."

"You had us."

"I did, but your mother wasn't very welcoming when I visited."

"I know. She isn't welcoming when anyone visits. Can we talk more about why you stopped coming?"

There were a few beats of silence while Aunt Alice looked like she was mulling over Charlotte's question.

"Your mother felt that I was having an undue influence on you. She called it my 'big city ways' and she didn't want me to convince you that the big city was for you."

"You never came back again."

"I didn't, but I talked to your dad every couple of months, just to see how you were doing."

"I didn't know that."

"We swore each other to secrecy. She would have made his life so miserable if she ever found out. I don't think she ever did."

"Dad never said a word. He was always so kind and patient. The very opposite of Mother."

"As I have said before, she was very lucky to find him in her life, very lucky he had the patience for her."

"Was she always like that? I know I've asked it before, but it's hard to understand someone being so miserable when they have so much."

"I know. She had a lovely daughter, a wonderful husband, no financial worries, and she didn't have to work. How could that have been bad?"

"Did she ever work?"

"Momma wouldn't have it. She said that women belonged in the home looking after their family. She made your mother work in the house and the garden and gave her an allowance for that. Begrudgingly, as I remember. She seemed to think she shouldn't have to pay her own children for helping around the house. I remember my dad telling her that Irene had a right to make some money, and if she couldn't get a job in town, then she should get paid for what she did at home."

"I don't remember Grandpa Knight."

"You wouldn't. He died just after you were born. He met you once, as I remember, and thought you were a genuine miracle."

"How did you get to go to university?"

"Oh, I knew early on that I would not be a farm wife. It looked like a lot of work for me. I helped your grandfather in the fields, driving the tractor, and feeding the animals. That way I was outside and away from Momma's critical tongue. My dad and I had lots of talks about life, and he kept me balanced. He also encouraged me to chase my dream."

"That's good to have. My dad was like that too. Interested in what I was interested in, always, and helping me to find out more." Charlotte said.

"I remember him telling me how proud he was when you graduated from high school and were accepted to university."

"It galled Mother when she found out he had saved money for my tuition. That and the scholarships I won gave me enough money to pay for the rest. She couldn't really deny me going based on money."

"You sound like me."

Charlotte smiled. She liked the sound of that. "Why did you pick accounting, Aunt Alice?"

"It was work that was necessary. If I had a family, I knew I could balance both more easily than with some of the other career choices. I liked math. Why did you choose it?"

"The same. Except I hadn't considered the family aspect. When I was choosing what to do, my dad once said that if I needed any advice, I could turn to you."

"You didn't."

"Didn't what?" Charlotte pinched her eyebrows together.

"Didn't turn to me."

"I never needed to. Until now. It came fairly easily, and when I graduated and got offered a job, I felt safe."

"Do you need advice now?"

"I don't know where to turn now. I've lost my job. I don't want to think that Mother was right. That I'm not much good for anything and I should just get married and be at home."

"She said that?"

"She did. When I applied to university. When I graduated. When I got my designation. Now she reminds me I still must pay rent, to look after her, as I promised my dad."

"She is unkind."

"I'm not sure why. I am her daughter, her only child. You would think she would be my champion. Be on my side."

"I guess she didn't think anyone gave her a break, so she won't give anyone else one, or let them have what they want, or be happy."

"Aren't you supposed to help family as much as you can?"

"I would, but maybe I have a different outlook than your mother."

"I wonder if Mother regrets not having a career, and a different life."

Aunt Alice twisted her head to look at Charlotte. "Does she ever say anything to you?" Charlotte felt Aunt Alice's eyes on her face, waiting for the answer—like it was of vital importance.

"About what? About her life? Not really. We don't talk about life or feelings, or really anything except rent and who is going to shovel the sidewalk in the winter." Charlotte thought for a moment and then added. "Do you think she regrets having me?"

"She never said so to me. Did she ever say anything to lead you to believe that?"

"Not really."

"Not really?"

"Well, she once said that I would never understand the responsibility having a child put on her shoulders. That it changed her entire life."

"Well, that is true about children. They change everything."

"She said it like she didn't have a choice. Surely pregnancy was a choice, even back then?"

"It was. Our generation was the first that could successfully control whether we had children. Your grandmother thought the pill would make all women loose even though I reminded her people had been having extra marital sex since forever. I remember she just snorted at me and told she would be keeping an eye on me when I brought boys around."

Charlotte giggled. "That's pretty overbearing."

"It was. I only brought one home. Momma looked at him like a tiger ready to pounce if he made a move. I never did that again. We met at the movies or the coffee shop instead. Although there weren't many that came around."

"Did she treat Mother that way too?"

"Yes, Irene said it felt like having two burning spots on your back when a boy was around the house." Alice laughed too.

"Wow, you guys had it tough."

"We did. But we were in it together, and somehow that made it okay. When we were teenagers, we'd lay in our beds and talk about what we were going to do with our lives."

"What did Mother say?" Charlotte's eyebrows raised. She didn't know anything about her mother's dreams.

"She once said she wanted to be a chef. I encouraged her because she had a knack in the kitchen that I never had. She could look in the fridge and figure out a meal without a recipe book. She knew just what spices to add and how much to make food taste superb."

"Mother's food is always excellent. Her baking makes you crave more. Was she allowed to go to college or university?"

"When she started making noises about going to the technical school to train, Momma had a fit. I had left for university by then, and I don't think Momma was about to lose her other daughter. Beatrice said Irene didn't have the head for learning that I did and said she would not be successful that way, but she sure could run a household well. She said her energy would be better spent getting married and being a farm wife."

"That must have been hard."

"It was awful. Irene called me that night and cried for a half hour on the phone. Momma wasn't letting her go anywhere, and so she got married. Your dad proposed out of the blue and she accepted. He had just taken over his parents' farm and had built a brand-new house. She got to choose new everything. Everyone was so jealous of her. I knew he had always loved her. I'm not so sure she felt the same about him. And then you came along, and everything changed. She became moody, unpredictable, unpleasant, and unhappy."

"I caused that?"

"I don't think so. I think it had to do with living up to Momma's standards. Irene seemed to enjoy motherhood, but Momma was demanding in her expectations of Irene as a mother and wife."

"Poor Dad. To get married to someone you love and not feel loved back."

"I think your father thought something he did made her unhappy. So, he worked harder, gave her more things, bought her jewelry and let her spend money as she wanted. He thought that would make her happy. It took a while, but he finally figured out that it wasn't anything he did. She chooses not to be happy. By then, her unhappiness was so habitual that he just figured out how to avoid her when she is in one of her moods and kept busy with the farm. Luckily he was a smart with cattle and they did well."

"They did, but they didn't seem happy. No smiles, no hugs, and no kisses. Which is worse? Financially well off and unhappy or poor but happy?"

"I'm not sure. I think there is a balance. You need to take the wheel of your life and not succumb to the directional signs of others."

"Grandma's signals."

"Yes, my mother's signals. She was a force. You didn't mess with her."

"So is my mother. She is a force." Charlotte said.

"Hence my thoughts. It is your life, Charlotte. You make all the choices for it and then hold yourself accountable for the results."

The squawk of seagulls overhead brought Charlotte back to the present. She looked at her aunt and then at the ocean. She quietly mulled their conversation over as they stood in line at the ice cream kiosk and ordered double cones.

Aunt Alice was right. It was the best ice cream in Canada.

twelve

. . .

"BACK TO THE shelter this morning, Charlotte. I'll let you loose in the office and maybe we can get you to walk Cocoa again." Aunt Alice and Charlotte were enjoying breakfast on the deck. The sky was blue, and the wind was light. Charlotte heard the barking of the seals on the shore. She inhaled the salty humidity of the ocean and thought she could easily live here. The thought surprised her. Moving out of her mother's house was a big enough leap; all the way to Victoria was a giant step.

"You are smiling again."

"I am."

"You're happy."

"I am. This is one of the first times I can remember enjoying a morning. No rush, and I am in love with the ocean. I might have to move here." Charlotte peered through her lashes at her aunt to see if there was a reaction. She didn't see one.

"You might as well live where you are happy. It makes little sense to live the one life you have in misery." Her aunt paused. "Can you be ready to go in ten minutes?"

"Sure, do I need anything different for today?"

"The usual, some comfortable shoes and clothes that you don't mind getting dirty. I can't guarantee where we walk will be dry since it rained last night."

"Okay, let me clean up the dishes. You go get ready." Charlotte took the dishes to the kitchen. She reflected on yesterday's conversation about her mother and her grandma. Seems that her mother didn't have a wonderful childhood. She felt some sympathy. But she couldn't reconcile why she would be as hard on her daughter as she was. Why wouldn't you want to rise above that and be a better parent with your child? Charlotte was pretty sure when and if she became a mother, she would show her child all the attention and unconditional love possible. She didn't want her child to feel as lost and ignored as she could remember feeling most of her life. Except when she was with her dad and her aunt.

The drive to the shelter took them out of the city on a narrow, windy road lined with trees. "I love this part of the island. Close to the city, but far enough away that you feel you are in another place entirely." Alice turned down the lane and pulled up to her parking spot along a fence.

"Does someone live on site?"

"No, but someone can stay if there is an animal in distress. There is a camera system online so we can check the animals. But we prefer to send the really hard cases to a foster home instead. Sandy does most of that. She lives about three minutes away. We lock the place at night. I think the animals have more peace with no humans around. But they are excited to see us in the morning."

Alice walked around the back of the house where dogs in five large open pens barked in greeting. "Don't mind them. Dogs bark for three reasons. They want you to know they know you are there, they are frightened, or they want some attention. These guys are saying good morning."

"Morning, Sandy." Alice greeted the woman with the twinkle in her eyes when they entered the kitchen. She was watching a little puppy put his nose into a bowl where there was some soft food. "How's Tyler this morning?"

Alice and Charlotte sat at the table.

"He's good. I think he's figuring food out. Finally."

"Well, he's a Lab. If it is one thing they know, it is how to eat." Alice and Sandy chuckled.

"Morning ladies. Glad you are here Charlotte. Your aunt could use someone to help her ease off a little while she is—"

Before Sandy could finish, Alice interrupted. "Don't listen to Sandy, or anyone else around here. They all think I work too hard."

Charlotte caught a look of something shared between Sandy and Alice but wasn't sure what it meant. "How many dogs do you have here?" she asked.

"Right now, we have twenty. That's about average. Sometimes we get a litter, then we are busy. I don't remember ever having fewer than ten."

"Not since I have been here," said Teresa, whose lipstick was more pink than red today. "But last month we had twenty-five from a poorly run puppy farm."

"Yeah, that made it crazy around here," said Bonnie. "But it was fun." Her smile warmed Charlotte's heart and made her feel welcome and accepted.

"Is the center an actual business or a nonprofit?" asked Charlotte.

"Oh, the center is a nonprofit but your aunt ..." started Teresa.

"Helps the nonprofit run by providing accounting and business management," Alice interrupted. "I am what they call an executive director. I alone handle the accounting, and we all do everything else. Right, ladies?" She looked at the others, who nodded in agreement.

"It must be hard to keep this afloat." Charlotte said.

"Oh, it is, but your aunt ..." Teresa started again.

"Has worked on non-profits before and knows how to

fundraise. So far we've been very successful." Alice finished again.

"Come on Charlotte. Let's go deal with the accounting." Charlotte felt her aunt's hand on her back, like she was being pushed. Charlotte noticed Teresa and Bonnie looking at each other when she said goodbye to them.

Aunt Alice took her to the office which was located across the hall from her aunt's. "So, my dear, here is the real reason I wanted you here. This is our accounting office." The pile of paper on the desk was as high as the computer. Charlotte hadn't noticed the piles the day before when she had peaked in. "Our bookkeeper left about three months ago, and I tried, but I can't keep up. I haven't had time to find a replacement. Then I thought of you. It offered an opportunity to bring you here and get to know you again and get this sorted out. When we get someone permanently, we can hand it over to them in a tidy state. I know it is asking a lot, but do you think you could try it?"

Charlotte looked at the piles of unopened envelopes, pieces of paper, and packages strewn all over the room. It was very much a mess. "Aunt Alice, I would love to. There is nothing I like to do better than to make simplicity and calm out of chaos."

"Oh, I'm happy to hear that. I'll get us a fresh pot of tea and find some cookies and leave you to get at it. Just dig in, there isn't anywhere specific to start. We tacked the passwords on the wall there. You are familiar with this accounting package?" Aunt Alice pointed to an icon on the computer screen.

"Very. Leave me to it. I'll have you sorted before you know it."

Charlotte sat in the chair and gazed around at the mayhem before her. It swelled her heart to see such a mess and know she could make it better. She sorted the paper, opened envelopes, and piled up dog food and toy samples in a basket she found in the corner. Page by page, she made sense out of what was in the room. She held the last envelope in her hand when she heard a noise and looked up, expecting to see her aunt with tea. She was ready for a cup.

Instead, she came face to face with an enormous dog, big by any standard. It stood in the doorway and only had to lift its head a little to look her in the eye. She was grateful for the desk in-between them. Her heart hammered in her ears. *Would it bite?* Her palms got sweaty. She wasn't sure what to do. *Could she get up and walk past it?* The dog drooled, and the slobber slipped out of its mouth and dropped by its feet. It panted. Charlotte remained still, put a tiny smile on her face to appear friendly. Her breathing increased in speed as her mind raced with what next to do.

"Shoo," she said as loudly as she could muster. But her voice was tight, and it came out as soft as a pigeon's coo.

thirteen

. . .

THE DOG CONTINUED TO PANT.

To her relief Charlotte heard footsteps in the hall. Aunt Alice negotiated her way around the dog in the doorway and placed the tea and cookies on the table near the window. "I see you have met Larry. He's our resident St. Bernard. Responsible for our safety, all the slobber you see around here, and as many walks as you would like to take."

"Hi Larry," Charlotte choked out. "He surprised me."

"He thinks he owns the place and has the run of it all. We only pen him during the night. He usually sits on the big pillow by the back door, but he must have been curious about you. Larry is harmless, but he is pretty big."

"He is and moves quietly." Charlotte stayed in her seat, not feeling at all safe to move, no matter how harmless Larry was.

"How are you doing with all this? Sorry it's such a fright, we've been just doing the bare necessities to get by." Aunt Alice's face begged for forgiveness.

"Oh, I've sorted the bills and the statements. It is not as bad as it first appears. I think I can have you up-to-date by the end of the week."

Alice's shoulders lowered, and a smile replaced her forlorn look. "Good. I knew you could help. One of our dog walkers called in sick today. Are you up for a dog walk later?"

Charlotte didn't feel she could say no. They discussed the time and Alice left Charlotte with her tea and work.

I'm not sure how I will handle this, she thought, *it might be okay but I'm still not sure. Can I get out of walking other dogs and walk Cocoa instead? Cocoa would be okay to walk.* She turned her attention to the papers before her, picked up the teacup and concentrated on sipping the tea instead.

———

The staff met in the lunchroom at noon, for a plate of sandwiches and cut up vegetables. Larry lay on a big pillow in the corner, fast asleep. Charlotte walked to an empty seat at the table on the opposite side of the room from Larry.

"So, Charlotte, you live in Beckerville?" Sandy's voice reminded her of bells at Christmas, a gentle tinkle sound.

"I do. Do you know it?"

"No. I'm afraid I have never left the island."

Charlotte nodded, knowing what that felt like. Before this, she had never left Beckerville, except to attend university and that didn't really count. "I have never been here before."

"What do you think?" Sandy asked.

"Oh, I love it. The air, the ocean, the birds, the green—all of it. It is so much more than Beckerville."

"We do have it lovely here. Perhaps that's why I've not left."

"Oh, come on, Sandy. We all know you haven't left because you have everything you want here. A beautiful home with plenty of acres for all those dogs you keep fostering." Everyone around the table laughed in agreement.

"I am pretty lucky. That's for sure. I guess when you find

what you want, you know enough to stay. I never had to look far for my happiness."

"Bonnie came to us after she moved to the island looking for another life." Alice turned to Bonnie for her confirmation.

"I did. I lived in Vancouver and, while I love the big city and all it offers, the noise, the people, the art, and the culture, I grew tired of the daily rush and the traffic. My apartment was near a busy road, and I could hear traffic and sirens all day long. Over two million people in a city make a lot of noise, I started getting anxiety attacks and not being able to function. There had to be a better way, so I packed up what I wanted, sold the rest, and moved here. I met Alice at the grocery store. She was friendly and had a kind smile. So different from my experience in the city." Bonnie gave Aunt Alice a grateful look. "She told me about this part-time job, and I got more part-time work at the grocery store. It surprised me to find lots of art and culture here too. Enough for me anyway. And at night, all I hear are the sounds of the wind and the animals. I am calmer and no more sleepless nights." She smiled at Alice.

"Don't look at me, Bonnie. I only gave you a job, the rest you did yourself. It takes a brave person to pack up their life and move to somewhere they have never lived to take better care of themselves."

"But if you hadn't given me this job, I wouldn't have been able to settle in so easily. Alice was the first person I met and asked me to stop by as soon as I could. It made all the difference." Bonnie said.

Alice bowed her head, blushing a little.

"We save more than just dogs around here," Bonnie admitted to Charlotte.

Charlotte smiled at her aunt. She liked her relative more and more.

Teresa arrived at the door to the lunchroom. "Hi folks. I know it's not my day to walk, but I had an afternoon off, and

I couldn't think of a place I would rather be. So put me to work."

"Well Charlotte, it looks like we won't need your help after all." Aunt Alice turned to Charlotte.

"I guess I'll go back to the books then." Charlotte hoped her face didn't show her relief. She headed back to the office, more than grateful for the rescue.

———

That night she shared the day with Janine on a video chat.

"You look well, Charlotte. I don't think I have ever seen you look so peaceful and serene. That place is good for you."

"Oh Janine, I feel like I have come home. I feel loved and accepted with my aunt. This part of the world is more lovely than I could have ever imagined. But ...," she paused. "There is only one slight problem."

"Oh, what could that be? Let me guess, your mother called, and she is going to visit you there?" Janine laughed as she made the comment.

"No, but I sure hope she doesn't come. That would ruin everything. It's just that the animal rescue place is all dogs. And you know how I feel about dogs."

"Well, that just goes to show you don't get it all. You'll be fine. It sounds like your aunt has a bunch of very experienced people there who will help you along. Ask for help. It will be okay."

"I'm sure it will, but I promised myself I would have nothing to do with dogs again after the incident with that dog, Bruce. What's worse, there's a Saint Bernard, just a little bigger than Bruce, that has the run of the place. The first time I met him I looked up from my desk and there he was, standing in the doorway looking at me. I almost fainted."

Janine laughed out loud. "Bruce was no shrimp either.

Nothing like getting into the deep end. Then what happened?"

"Well, I couldn't go anywhere. He was blocking the door, looking like he was going to eat me. But my aunt came in to drop off tea and took Larry back out with her."

"Larry. His name is Larry? Wasn't that the name of the boy you liked so much in school that wouldn't have anything to do with you?"

"Don't remind me."

"But you are going to have to face your fears I think."

"I am."

"Well, good luck to you. You look good. We'll talk about me the next time we chat." And she laughed again. "I've got to run. Everyone's waiting for me to tuck them in."

"Bye Janine, love you." Charlotte clicked the call off and sat looking at her aunt's computer, feeling warmed by a conversation with her best friend. She would miss Janine if she moved to the island.

Charlotte shook her head in wonderment at the thought. She hadn't consciously considered moving further away from her mother than somewhere else in Beckerville. Moving to the island was a big undertaking, but the more she thought about it, the more she liked the idea.

She went to bed thinking about the possibilities of a new life near her aunt.

fourteen

. . .

AUNT ALICE PARKED the car at the center early the next day. "Why don't we spend an hour together now, to learn more about gaining a dog's trust?" Aunt Alice asked.

"Are you sure I'm ready?"

"I know you are. You need some skills for handling these dogs. They are often abused or neglected or both. You need to approach them in a way that they can learn to trust you."

Charlotte wasn't sure whether to confess her fears or to just see how things went. But she could feel her heartbeat speeding up and the sweat beading on her brow, so she figured she better say something.

"Aunt Alice?"

"Charlotte."

"I have something you should know."

"What's that?"

"I'm afraid of dogs."

Aunt Alice gave her a look of concern, not pity or dismissal like her mother would have done. "Well, let's talk about it and see if we can help you with that. I figured something was up, Charlotte, I know fear on a person's face. The way you looked at Larry yesterday I thought you were going to jump out the window."

"Well, he is big."

"He is, but gentle. We kept him because once we had him settled down, we realized what a teddy bear he is. He takes up a lot of room and he sheds. Not really selling features for adoption and he is such a lovely face to see in the morning. Tell me what happened to you."

"I was small, about ten. Mom had a friend visiting who owned a mutt, a big one. His name was Bruce."

"No idea what breed?"

"No. Just big. I didn't know he was at our house. He ran up to me, licked my face and rubbed against me. Then he jumped on me, put his paws on my chest."

"What did your mother and the owner do?"

"Nothing. They thought he was so cute because he was being so friendly. They told me he was showing me how much he liked me. He was so big I felt like I was being pushed over but I was too scared to move away. I started crying because I didn't know what to do. When I finally moved, he bit me."

"Did it break skin?"

"Yes. Not a big cut but it bled. I thought I might need stitches, but my mother and the owner just laughed and said he was playing."

"Were you able to stop bleeding?"

"Yes, a little pressure and a tissue and it was good. I guess I overreacted."

"Oh, I doubt that. What did the owner do?"

"She told him to lay down."

"And did he?"

"Sort of, he wanted to play more, but she finally tugged on his collar, and he sat and then laid down. Then they wanted me to pet him, to show him everything was okay. As if I was the biter, but I wouldn't. He scared me so much that I couldn't even touch him. And then he barked. That's when I left. I never saw him again, but I veer a long way around any other dog I've seen since."

"Most dogs are generally friendly. However, if they have been treated badly, they can be defensive with strangers. I'd like to think that Bruce was being overly friendly. But if no one helped you deal with him, then the blame lies with the owner for not controlling her dog. I'm sorry that was your experience. Dogs can be such good companions and so loving. Let me show you some techniques for approaching dogs that will make them less anxious about you. I'm not guaranteeing that you won't have any problems, but with a different approach you might find dealing with them easier." Aunt Alice showed Charlotte how to hold her hand when greeting a dog, how to talk to them, and what to do when they didn't behave in an appropriate manner.

"Think you do can this?"

"I think so," said Charlotte.

"Good. Remember that it might not work the first time but be persistent. Let's go find Cocoa and see if we can't build your confidence. Sandy said she was going to take some dogs out."

"Sandy, can Charlotte walk dogs with you?"

"Sure. Come on Charlotte, it's a nice day for a walk."

Sandy had several leashes clipped to one cage. Charlotte watched as she unclipped one leash and opened the cage that contained a brown and white dog. She made approaching and leashing the dog look easy. She moved to a second pen to do the same with another dog that looked very similar.

"Charlotte, I'm going to take Barney for a walk. Once I have you set up with Fred, you can follow. Keep some distance between us so that the dogs don't excite each other," Sandy said.

"Aren't I going to walk, Cocoa?"

"No, she's already gone with Bonnie. This is Fred." Sandy

handed Charlotte a leash. "He and Barney are brothers. They need to know who is boss, so keep a good hold on the leash. They have walked this path a million times so they can lead you."

"Um, thanks." Charlotte tentatively took the leash and felt the slight tug of the dog. She held her other hand out and let Fred sniff it in introduction. She waited while he sniffed it thoroughly and then turned her hand slowly and rubbed the side of his face.

"Hi Fred. How about we have a pleasant walk?" Fred pulled Charlotte along gently, as Sandy had promised. He walked down one side of the path, stopped, sniffed the ground, and then, distracted by a smell on the other side of the path, moved there to sniff.

Hmm, I think I can do this. Charlotte relaxed a little and talked to Fred about the trees and bushes as they walked.

Suddenly, he tugged hard on the leash. Charlotte wasn't ready for it, and before she knew it, the leash and Fred had disappeared after a squirrel. She realized she had not held the leash as tight as Sandy had instructed. Muttering to herself at her incompetence, she ran after the dog, yelling his name. She only caught up to him because he had tired of chasing the squirrel when it ran up a tree. He was standing beside his brother.

"Oh Charlotte, are you all right?" Sandy asked.

"I'm afraid I failed my first walk."

"Oh, don't worry. I should have taken them both myself. They like to walk together, but we thought Fred would be a good starter dog for you."

"I'm so sorry. I'm glad nothing bad happened."

"Not much bad can happen around here. High fences encircle the property so, even if all the dogs got loose, the fence would pen them in. We don't want them out in the neighborhood, so the fence protects the dogs and the neigh-bors. There was some opposition to a dog shelter here because people thought there would be rabid Rottweilers running around all the time. It took some time, but we have convinced people we are responsible dog caregivers. And the fence helped. In fact, most of volunteer walkers are local retired people. Both need company and a walk. It's been a fortunate coincidence."

"Still, I am glad nothing happened."

"Don't be so hard on yourself. Your aunt wouldn't put you in a position where you could be harmed. She loves you." Sandy bent to pick up Fred's leash and handed it to Charlotte. "Come on, we can walk together."

They finished up the walk around the property without further incident.

"How did it go?" Aunt Alice was on the doorstep when they arrived at the center.

"I failed," admitted Charlotte.

"At what?"

"I let the leash go and Fred ran away."

"And then?"

"And then I caught up with him. He was standing beside Barney with Sandy."

"So, everything is okay."

"Well, yes. But I didn't maintain control over Fred."

"But you tried. And Fred is easy. Better to fail on an easy one and build some skills. We'll get you to walk again." She put her arm around Charlotte and led her back to the house. "Come on, it's time for lunch."

Charlotte spent the afternoon in the office, working through the various capabilities of the accounting software to make daily work more efficient. She was printing out the last month's financial statements when she heard a noise in the hallway. Hoping it wasn't Larry, she bravely poked her head out of the office.

"Hello," she offered.

"Oh, hello." A young woman wearing a tattered coat and

rubber boots stood in the hallway. "I'm Renee. I live just down the way. On my way into town, I found a dog in a box in the ditch. It looks like she just had a litter. I can't take her because I have young kids and my hands are full."

"Let me get someone who can help you." Charlotte did not know where everyone was, but she was sure she should find someone with more experience.

"Sorry, I hate to dump and run, but I have a couple of appointments in the city that I can't be late for. Can't I just give them to you?"

"Well, sure." Charlotte's stomach was turning like an electric mixer used for making batter. "Let's go look."

Renee opened the hatch on her SUV, where an auburn-colored dog huddled on a ratty blanket in a box. She had three very tiny puppies tucked next to her. Renee looked at Charlotte, expecting her to do something. Charlotte put her hand into the box with her fingers curled in, like her aunt had shown her. The dog immediately snapped at her with a snarl. Charlotte pulled her hand back quickly, not sure what to do next.

"Why don't you grab one side of the box?" Charlotte suggested. "I'll grab the other and we can carry them into the house."

"Sure, I can help with that, but then I have to go." The woman looked as nervous as Charlotte felt.

Charlotte hoped the box would hold the dogs until they got them inside the center. They lifted the box and the dogs gently out of the car and carried it inside the house to the kitchen floor.

"Thanks. If I get a chance, I'll stop by and check on them. They sure are cute. Here's my name and number." Renee scribbled on a piece of paper from her pocket and handed it to Charlotte. She backed out of the door, leaving Charlotte standing, staring at the dogs, wondering what to do next.

Charlotte dug into the cupboard that held the dog dishes

and poured some water into a bowl and placed it in the box. Not knowing what else to do, she sat down beside the dogs and murmuring to the mother, asked her where she was from. Charlotte's voice seemed to soothe the dog, and she fell asleep.

That's where Aunt Alice found Charlotte. "Oh my, what is this?"

"A woman found them in the ditch. She couldn't take them so dropped them off here. Here is her name and number."

Aunt Alice bent down to look closer at the contents of the box after she tucked the note into her pocket. "Well, the poor things."

"I didn't know what to do, so I gave her some water and waited."

"Perfect. I'll go set up a shelter for her." Aunt Alice paused at the door. "You'll be okay?"

"I'll just sit here. I showed her my hand before, but she snapped at me."

"Protective mother. And probably scared. She'll come around."

Alice was back ten minutes later. "Let's get them settled in the pen. The mother looks like she could use something to eat." They carried the box to a pen where a heater was turned on low to warm the space.

"It'll give them a boost if we give them some heat for a couple of days. Bring me a bowl of food for her, and that water bowl you had while I figure out how to get them out of this box and that awful blanket."

With the bowl of food in hand, Charlotte watched her aunt quietly cut down the sides of the box so that it lay flat. Then she arranged the fresh blankets right beside the old box, put the water and food dishes nearby, and shut the gate of the pen.

"There, that'll give them some space, and she will move

them when she is ready. Let's just leave them. We can check on them when we go home. But I think they will be fine. I'll have Tim come look at them tomorrow."

"Tim?"

"He's the vet and works with us on all our dogs. He's a gem, has a way with dogs that have little trust in humans."

Later that afternoon, Charlotte cast one more look at the poodle in the pen. The dog looked up at Charlotte. Her eyes seemed to soften. Charlotte wanted to think it was in thanks. She would be sure to visit the dog and her pups every day.

fifteen

. . .

THEY TALKED about the box of dogs on the way to the center the next morning.

"That new dog sure seems scared," Charlotte observed.

"We see a lot of that. The puppies are her priority, and she doesn't know this new world she has been thrust into."

"What will happen to her?"

"We will feed and care for her and the puppies and then arrange for their adoption. Like we do with others. Would you like to help with her?"

"I would. She showed me her fear by snapping at me, I know that. But I thought she looked at me kindlier when I left last night. I don't feel so scared of her like I feel with other dogs."

"We make connections with different beings for different reasons. Perhaps you have something to learn from each other. On another topic, how is the accounting coming?"

"Oh, I am all finished."

"Already? Everything is up-to-date?"

"Yes. I'll print off current statements, we can go over them when you have time."

"Sure, let's do it first thing. Thank you, Charlotte, I hadn't expected you to be done so fast."

"I really like organizing and cleaning up things, getting them up to date. The accounts just needed some attention paid to them. Easy."

"Easy for you to say."

Charlotte smiled at her aunt.

They arrived at the center ten minutes later. Charlotte peeked in at the new mom and her puppies sleeping on the fresh blanket. She returned to the office where she and her aunt went through the documents.

"Charlotte, this is really outstanding work. You have set up the monthly payments and calendar reminders of important dates for us. The computer system was just updated, and I haven't had the time to finish the setup. This is way beyond what I expected. Thank you. You should do these books, not me."

"Actually, I was wondering if you would mind if I stayed on another week. I'll keep the accounts up to date, and I want to spend time with the new dog and her puppies. And maybe I can help walk Fred and Barney as well."

"I wouldn't mind at all. You are always welcome at my home. Why don't I leave you to change your flight? Does your mother know?" Aunt Alice didn't wait for an answer, nodded at Charlotte, and left the office.

The flight arrangement was simple. Charlotte happily paid the change fee because it gave her an extended stay. She paused before she dialed her mother's number. She wasn't sure what to expect for a response, but this was really a courtesy call.

"Hello, Mother."

"Charlotte, are you home already? Did all those dogs chase you away?" Irene's laugh had a sharp edge to it, like broken glass.

"No, the dogs and I are getting along just fine. I'm calling to let you know I am staying on another week."

"What do you mean? You can't be spending your time walking dogs and getting friendly with your aunt when you need to be looking for a job."

"Mother, I'm paid up. I'm not sure what else can matter to you." Charlotte surprised herself with her pushback. Obviously staying with her aunt was doing her confidence some good.

"You will regret this, Charlotte Irene Martin. Don't say I didn't warn you." And the call ended.

Charlotte shrugged her shoulders after she hung up the phone. Typical reaction from her mother. She stood and then remembered she needed to call Janine. She felt drawn to the new dog and puppies, so she decided that call could wait for the evening. Charlotte realized they would have to give the dog a name; she couldn't go around calling her the new dog. She thought about possible names as she walked to the pen.

She found Sandy in the pen, gently trading more clean blankets for dirty ones and mopping up puppy pee. "Charlotte, just in time. Can you go fill these bowls with food and find out from your aunt when Tim will be here?"

Charlotte returned with the food and water and announced that Tim would arrive in about ten minutes.

"Good. I think everything is good here. They look like they had a good night, but I'll be more certain about them when Tim has had a look."

Charlotte quietly stepped into the pen and put the food and water down. She slowly moved her closed fist toward the dog's nose and held it still while the mother dog sniffed. There wasn't a snap this time, and Charlotte's heart lightened. She was glad she had extended her visit.

She turned to the noise of people coming toward the pen and saw a tall man with dark, curly hair and light-grey, kind eyes making his way to the pen with her aunt.

"Tim, this is my niece, Charlotte. She is here for a visit and to help us out."

"Glad to meet you, Charlotte."

Charlotte had never seen anyone carry their confidence so easily. The men she worked with were intense and analytical, outstanding characteristics for an accountant, but not what she was looking for in a partner. She blushed that she was thinking about a partner as they shook hands. She was grateful he didn't seem to notice her flushed face.

"A pleasure to meet you, Tim."

"Let's have a look, shall we?"

He made his way to the pen and lowered himself down to the dog's level.

"Why are you crouching down?"

"When you are meeting dogs, especially for the first time, getting down to their level helps build comfort and a little trust."

The puppies had awakened and were moving around, looking blindly for milk.

"These pups are pretty new. Their eyes haven't even opened yet."

He let the mother sniff his hand and then she allowed him to stroke her head as he whispered to her. "It's okay little one, you are safe here. Does she have a name?"

Charlotte's eyes teared at his words—such kindness. He obviously had a touch because the dog easily let him rub her all over. "I think we should call her Lucy." Charlotte replied and looked to her aunt for approval.

Aunt Alice nodded. "A fine name. Tell Charlotte what you are doing Tim."

"As I stroke her, I feel all of her body to make sure there is nothing wrong." He finished his inspection and rose from the crouched position. "Charlotte, I think that Lucy just needs some rest and food. This brood will keep her busy for a while yet, but there is no reason to believe she won't be fine. Now let's have a look at the pups."

He lifted each one up and gently felt around their bodies.

"Three males. Everything looks good here. Lucy will need a break from them every day, so you can take her for a short walk or put her in an outside pen. Once they have opened their eyes, they can go with her to the outside pen. They will sleep a lot, so walk her when they are sleeping. I'll get Sandy to set up appointments for their shots and call you. I can tell someone cared for her, her coat is shiny. She is just lean because she is feeding three hungry little boys."

"Why would someone abandon them in a ditch?"

"Some people would rather offload their problems than look for places like the center to help them out." He took one last look at the pups, walked out of the pen and shut the gate. "They don't realize the full responsibility they have with a pet. If they don't want pups, they should get them spayed or neutered so there won't be more puppies. Abandoning their problem is just not a mature solution."

"Do you have time for tea, Tim?" Aunt Alice called from the door.

"I think I can fit one in, if you have some of those wonderful cookies." He winked at Aunt Alice.

"Hobnobs? We always have Hobnobs. They are on our weekly grocery list, like dog food and toilet paper." Aunt Alice laughed.

Over hot tea, a plate full of cookies, and lots of laughter around the table, Tim told the latest story of adventures at his vet clinic.

"We had a Lab pup in the other day. You know they are notorious for eating anything and everything." Tim looked around the table as everyone nodded. "Well, this poor dog was lethargic and drinking lots. The owners were very concerned because he was usually such a rambunctious puppy. We looked him over but could only feel a strangely full stomach, almost like he had eaten lead. So, we x-rayed him and found a lump. Of course, we were concerned that it was not a normal lump." Again, everyone nodded. "But we had to operate because there was no other way to get the obstruction to move."

"What did it turn out to be?" Asked Aunt Alice.

"Turns out the dog was in the chicken coop and ate a lot of chicken feed. We cleaned it all out, and he went home wagging his tail."

"So like a Lab to eat anything that looks like food." They all laughed.

"Now Charlotte? What's your story? What brings you to the island?" Tim asked.

"Well, my aunt invited me for a visit," she started.

"She is updating our accounting records, and is helping with the dogs," Alice finished.

"When do you go back?"

"I actually just extended my visit for another week; I just lost my job." It surprised Charlotte she was so vulnerable.

"Well, nothing like a shock to make you take stock and decide what you really want." That comment, made with no judgement and Tim's manner with the dogs made her trust him. She watched as he chatted easily with the women around the table. What a charming human being. Her aunt sure knew good people.

"Say Alice, are we still on for sailing this weekend?"

"We are Tim. Saturday, right?"

"Charlotte, are you up for some sailing?"

Charlotte looked at her aunt and Tim. "I've never sailed."

Aunt Alice's eyes were kind. "That's not what we asked."

"Yes, I'm up for some sailing."

"Well then, come along, find out what sailing on the ocean is like. Your aunt will fill you in. Listen, I must go, other animals are waiting. See you both on Saturday." Tim was up and gone.

Charlotte wasn't sure if she was excited or scared about sailing. She wondered about the smile shared by her aunt and the others round the table, as she left to go out to the puppies.

sixteen

. . .

"AUNT ALICE, is your hairdresser any good?"

"Of course, Charlotte. How do you think I look this pretty?" Aunt Alice laughed with a joy Charlotte was getting used to hearing.

"Are you always this happy, Aunt Alice?"

"Happiness is a choice, Charlotte. No matter what is going on in your world, you have control over how you respond to it. I choose to be happy because it is easier and leaves fewer wrinkles." Aunt Alice laughed. "What did you have in mind for your hair, Charlotte?"

"Shorter hair and maybe some new clothes."

"Then let's plan a day. I'll see if my salon has an opening this morning and let the center know we won't be coming in."

Charlotte got her hair cut and had highlights added. It softened her face and made her smile seem brighter. The difference was surprising. She usually spent little time on her appearance. She reflected on the first time she tried makeup on herself.

A boy from junior high had asked her to go to the movies. She had stroked a wand of mascara on her lashes to make them just a little more noticeable and brushed blue eyeshadow over her eyelids to look like she had seen in a magazine. She had applied a soft pink lipstick to her lips and smacked them.

Her mother saw her putting on her coat. "Where are you going and why are you wearing makeup?"

"Someone has invited me to go to the movies."

"Charlotte, you need to accept the facts. You are not pretty. Look at you. I'm surprised this boy asked you out. He must be desperate."

"But he asked Mother. And I want to go."

"Well, I will not let you. You are still a minor and I still have authority over you."

"You make it sound like I am in prison."

"You are under my control until you turn eighteen. And I'm saying you can't go."

"But Mother."

"Charlotte, there is no discussion. Now go take that makeup off your face and change your clothes. There is some housework you can tend to instead."

Since then, no one had asked her out, and she only spent time with Janine. She graduated high school without going to the graduation dance. No one asked, and she figured that her mother wouldn't let her go, anyway. She became an expert at being invisible and not drawing attention to herself.

Charlotte looked at her new hair and clothes and thought about those days and her mother's words. Her mother was wrong. She was pretty. Why hadn't she *seen* herself before?

Aunt Alice stilled when she exited the change room. "Charlotte," she whispered. "You look amazing."

Charlotte turned to her reflection. She grinned. Her heart grew in her chest three sizes bigger. "I know."

Aunt Alice laughed out loud.

Charlotte floated out of the store on a cloud of what she thought might be happiness. It was like there were new hues to the spectrum. She felt taller, more capable, and lighter.

Happy was a feeling she was unfamiliar with, and feeling it made her uncomfortable. Did she deserve to feel happy from a few clothes and a new haircut? Or was something else going on? She tried to shake off the discomfort and tell herself it was okay to feel this way.

They stopped at one of her aunt's favorite bistros for a late lunch.

"Charlotte, we come into this world worthy of love and kindness. No matter what, we are worthy of love, even though it may not come from the sources we expect. For you, some highlights and new clothes have made you look at yourself differently. And your work with the dogs has changed you too." Aunt Alice paused, as if choosing her words carefully. "Time away from your mother may have helped as well."

"What do you mean?"

"When you arrived here, you looked like you were checking over your shoulder for a ghost. Every day since, you stand a little taller, believe in yourself a little more."

"You noticed."

"Charlotte, I know that with kindness comes easing and acceptance. And that time heals most wounds."

Charlotte's eyes filled with tears. "Aunt Alice, you've shown me you can choose to be happy, despite what is going on around you."

"You got that did you? Really, I've shown you an option. The choice is yours. Believe me, good things are yet to come to you."

They hugged in the longest hug Charlotte had ever had. Nothing more needed to be said.

Charlotte and her aunt climbed into her Jetta and made their way home to spend the next few hours walking on the beach path.

seventeen

. . .

TWO DAYS LATER, Charlotte was brave and walked Fred and Barney by herself. It was a sunny day and felt like a great day for a walk with dogs. She planned they would take the loop right down to the dock and then run back to get rid of some of their restless energy. She had seen how Sandy handled them and saw how well they walked together. Her walks with Cocoa had gone well too, so she was feeling more confident with dogs. She figured she could do it and told her aunt so.

Aunt Alice looked at Charlotte over her glasses, as was her habit. "Are you sure, Charlotte?"

"I think I can handle them, when they are together."

"Well then, let's try it."

Charlotte tucked treats into her pocket in case she needed to coax them to cooperate. She took their leashes off the labelled hook in the porch and clipped Barney's to the mesh of his pen while she handled Fred. She easily slipped the collar over his head and snapped the leash to the collar. She hung Fred's leash around a post while she readied Barney and then grasped both leashes in her hands and headed down the path. She smiled at how easy it had been and almost laughed at how crazy the first times had been. *Why had it felt so hard?*

A few yards down the path, Charlotte noticed Sandy following with the stray they named Rex. Charlotte wasn't sure if she followed out of concern for her lack of experience, or just as a matter of course with new walkers, but it relieved her she was there.

The walk started out easy. The dogs strained on the leashes in front of her, causing Charlotte to tighten her grip. But they settled into an even pace, so her mind shifted to sailing later that day. The sky was blue, and the breeze was light. She hoped that meant easy sailing. Charlotte didn't have a lot of experience around water, so was a little nervous. The ocean was a big space. She tempered her fears by reminding herself that her aunt would keep her safe.

Her attention returned to the dogs as they jumped and nipped at each other. She allowed them this fun and smiled, not realizing that sometimes this game escalates. Without notice, the dogs were straining fully at the leashes and jumping up and down on their hind legs, nipping at each other with jaws wide open. Then Barney jumped on top of Fred, chomping at his face and neck. To Charlotte it looked like they were fighting. She pulled back on Barney's leash in her left hand while easing off the one on her right. She hoped that would put some distance between the dogs. But it didn't work. The situation was out of her control. She called their names, hoping to divert their attention. "Fred. Barney. Now stop this." She turned around to look for Sandy, hoping for a rescue.

"Fred. Barney." Sandy shouted sternly at the dogs, as she caught up to Charlotte. She handed Charlotte Rex's leash and told him to sit. He sat down to watch the show. "Charlotte, stayed with Rex. I'll get these two sorted. Come on, you two. Time for play is now over." Sandy bent over and grabbed

Barney by the scruff of the neck and pulled him off Fred. She commanded him to sit, and he did.

"Now let's get you two calmed down a bit before we return to the pens."

Sandy turned to Charlotte. "Are you all right?"

"I think so. Sorry, I was getting ahead of myself. I thought I was ready for more."

"No worries. Those two are rambunctious sometimes and you must monitor and adjust all the time. They were just playing, no harm done."

"That's the first time I've seen that. I thought they were fighting."

"It's just dogs playing. Come on, you two. Time to get back. Charlotte, you go on ahead of me with Rex."

Sandy didn't say another word, and Charlotte quietly returned to the center. She felt like she had failed and decided she would not walk dogs again. In fact, she was pretty sure she should just return to her home in Beckerville and forget the island altogether. She knew her aunt was going to be disappointed in her. She was disappointed in herself.

eighteen

. . .

ALICE MET Charlotte in the center's kitchen. "Tough day heh?"

"You could say that."

"Well, if you don't try, you don't learn. Grab your bag and we'll walk to the dock."

"Aunt Alice, I'm not sure I should try sailing. I doubt I would be any good at it."

"I'm sure you will be terrible, but you have to start somewhere."

Charlotte stared at her aunt in disbelief. She couldn't believe what she heard.

"Oh Charlotte, it'll be fine. It's a lovely day, with enough wind to move us but not blow us around. Let's have an enjoyable afternoon and forget about dogs for a while."

———

On the dock, they paused beside the boat and Aunt Alice pointed out some of its parts. "Always one hand for you and one for the boat. There are life jackets below, one for each of us. We always wear them."

Tim was already on the boat, taking coverings off. "Hi ladies. Great day for sailing I think."

"I think so too, Tim. Charlotte, go down and grab the life jackets on the front settee."

Charlotte gently stepped onto the boat and made her way gingerly down the steep steps to what her aunt called the salon. The boat rocked slightly, and she grabbed anything to keep herself steady. Tim and Aunt Alice chatted happily on deck while she looked around her.

In front of her was a set of open doors, behind which she could see V-shaped spaced, lined with several cushions that fit perfectly. A small kitchen with a two-burner stove and sink was to her left. To the right was a small table with maps on it. She peeked behind the stairs where there was a small bathroom and another space that looked like it was used for storage. Its ceiling was low and stretched the width of the boat.

Her orientation downstairs gave her time to gather herself and find the brave face she needed to get through the afternoon. She was feeling downhearted from the dog episode. This whole adventure on the island was perhaps beyond her abilities, and going sailing was foolish. But here she was. She climbed back up to the deck with her life jacket on and handed Aunt Alice and Tim theirs.

Aunt Alice clipped on her jacket and stepped behind the big wheel. "The wind is low here in the bay, so we will motor out to the inlet to set the sails there. Have a seat here in the cockpit. I'll take us out."

The wheel was at the back of the cockpit and benches ran along both sides of the boat between the wheel and the hatch Charlotte had entered to get the life jackets. Charlotte sat down on one side. Aunt Alice started the motor. Tim was unwrapping the lines at the front and the back of the boat that tied it to the dock. As he lifted the last line off the dock he said, "Ready Alice."

Aunt Alice put the engine in reverse and backed the boat

into the inlet. Tim took the lines, wrapped them in loops, and tossed them into the salon below. Aunt Alice shifted the motor into forward gear and the boat headed toward where the water widened.

"There are no ropes on the boat, Charlotte, there are lines, halyards, and sheets depending on their purposes. The ones that tie us to the dock are lines. The ones that pull up sails, or hoist them, are called halyards, and the ones that control sails are called sheets." Tim made it sound simple to remember.

Charlotte shook her head wondering how she would ever remember this new language.

Tim busied himself pulling up rubber cylinders that hung alongside the boat on the outside. "These are fenders. They protect the sides of the boat when it is at the dock." He dropped them down to the salon with the lines. "I'll tidy all that up once we are sailing." He winked at her.

Once they left the bay, the shorelines spread far to the left and to the right. The world spread open before them. The water stretched to a far shore that rose from the water to treed hills. The ocean stretched in both directions to unseen waterways.

"Charlotte, come here," her aunt beckoned.

Charlotte rose and gripped her way along to where her aunt stood behind the wheel.

"Tim and I are going to raise the sails. I need you to keep the boat pointed that way."

Charlotte felt her stomach tighten and a little sweat on her forehead. "I can't do that."

"Why ever not?" Aunt Alice turned. "Charlotte, trust me. I wouldn't ask of you something I didn't think you could handle."

"I've never done this before. What if something happens?"

"Nothing will happen. Just keep the boat pointed in that direction. See that grey dock sticking out from shore over there?" Alice pointed to a dock in front of them on the far shore.

"I have shifted the engine to neutral. There is no wind. Nothing will happen. Just hang on to the wheel."

"Okay, just hang on to the wheel," Charlotte repeated, to make herself sure.

Tim and Alice worked together, standing on the deck at the front of the boat. Tim named boat parts and described what they were doing as they went. They loosened straps that held a sail to the boom, a short metal pole attached perpendicular to the bottom of the mast.

"This is the mainsail." He pointed to the sail they had just freed from the straps. "The mainsail gives us the power to sail. We only raise it when the boat points into the wind, so that the wind won't fill it and make it hard to raise. That's why you are there, to keep us pointed into the wind." He pointed to an arrow at the top of the mast. "That arrow points into the wind. Keep it pointed forward while we put up the sail. Once the mainsail is raised, we will turn the boat so that the sail can fill, and we will start moving." He snugged the halyard he used to raise the mainsail into a clamp and stepped back into the cockpit.

Alice replaced Charlotte at the helm. She turned the motor off and gently turned the wheel to the left. The sails filled. The boat moved forward. Charlotte watched in amazement.

Tim and Charlotte now sat across from each other on the boat. He pointed to a sail lying on the deck at the bow of the boat. "That is the jib sail. And this is its halyard." He lifted the halyard out of a clamp and pulled on it. "The jib connects to the bow of the boat and near the top of the mast. That corner of it that is nearest to us is called the clew. It has two lines, or sheets attached to it. One for each side of the boat. The sheets are wrapped around the winches on each side to help tighten them. The jib lies on one side of the boat or another, depending on where the wind is coming from." He wrapped the sheet on his side of the boat around a winch in front of him and instructed Charlotte to unwrap the sheet from the winch on her side.

Charlotte watched as the smaller triangular-shaped sail rose the front of the mast. Tim snugged the halyard into a clamp and looked at the jib. He tugged on the rope wrapped around the winch on his side and Charlotte watched the edges of the sail tighten up and felt the boat move forward a little faster.

"Let's see what the ocean looks like today." Aunt Alice said from the helm.

The boat tipped over to the left side just a little and Charlotte adjusted herself to feel more comfortable with the angle. She was glad of the new sunglasses to protect her eyes from the sun's glare off the water. She realized she was enjoying herself by the calm that overtook her and the smile she found herself wearing as she let the wind lift and pull on her hair. The salty tang of the ocean helped her let go of the dog events of the morning. She looked at Tim and Alice to see if they were having as much fun as she was.

"How about we go to Maple Bay today?" Aunt Alice suggested.

"Is there enough time? We only have the afternoon." Tim said.

"I think so. The wind is in our favor, and we always have the motor."

They maintained a consistent distance from the shore, sailing parallel to it, enjoying steady winds, and making obvious progress. They spent an hour talking about sailing in the area. Charlotte noticed other boats on the water and thought how lucky they all were to enjoy the day this way.

"Anyone hungry?" Tim went down below without waiting for an answer. She saw him lift the lines and fenders he had tossed down earlier and hang them on hooks. Tim returned to the deck with a zipped bag. From it he handed out a sandwich and a small bag of potato chips to each of them. "Here's a bottle of water as well. Sailing dehydrates you more than you would think."

Charlotte noticed Tim kept scanning in front of the boat and then around them as he ate his sandwich. He noticed her watching him and said, "I'm just checking for stuff in the water ahead of the boat that might damage it and monitoring for other boats, to make sure we aren't on a collision course with them. Things happen fast so you want to keep watch."

She started looking for boats and things on the water as she sipped her drink.

"Tim, time for you to take over." Aunt Alice stepped to the side of the wheel, still hanging on to it.

"Are you feeling okay?" Tim said as he replaced Aunt Alice at the helm.

Charlotte thought Tim looked concerned, but her aunt's immediate shake of her head lessened her worry. "Don't be silly, Tim. I'm just fine. I would just like to sit and enjoy my lunch."

She sat down, opened her sandwich, and smiled at Charlotte as she took a bite. Tim steered them on their way. They chatted about the various places around this bay that they had seen in their sailing travels.

Aunt Alice looked at her watch. "I think we should let Charlotte have a turn at the helm," she said.

"Oh, I'm happy sitting here pulling sheets," Charlotte assured them. "I don't need a turn on the helm."

"Well, I think differently. I think you should. Just for a bit. Tim can take us into the dock." Aunt Alice's voice was firm.

Charlotte and Tim traded places. Aunt Alice remained sitting in the cockpit finishing her sandwiches. "Now, Charlotte, it is easy. Just stand here and hold the wheel. Look at something on a far shore, in the direction you want to head. See that red roof?"

"That one?" She tried to sound sure as she pointed to a red roof on a distant shore, but inside she was nervous.

Aunt Alice nodded in agreement. Charlotte steered for the red roof. Tim told her to turn the wheel a little to the left and a little to the right, back and forth, to keep them on course. It provided a slight rocking of the boat but easily maintained progress straight toward the red roof.

"It works," she exclaimed in surprise.

"There is nothing static about sailing. You must check and adjust all the time. Get into that habit and you'll be okay."

Charlotte felt the wind on her face and breathed in the fresh air. It calmed her nervousness. So far, it seemed easy, but she would not let down her guard. That's where she had gone wrong with the dogs. She had let down her guard, and she had failed. That would not happen again.

"Let's turn to go that way," said Alice. She pointed ninety degrees to the right of their current heading.

"Well, someone come up here and I'll pull sheets." Charlotte almost walked away from the helm.

"No, you stay there."

"But I can't."

"You can," Tim said. "Just keep doing what you have been doing. Look over your right shoulder. Find a new point to aim for. Got one?"

Charlotte nodded.

"What are you pointing at?"

"That white boat over there." Charlotte pointed to a boat near the shore to her right.

"Is it underway?"

Charlotte turned a puzzled face to Tim.

"Is it moving? If it is moving, then you can't use it to steer toward."

"How can you tell if it is moving?"

"Watch it for a while. If the land behind it changes, then it is moving. If the land behind it stays the same, then the boat is not in motion. Is it moving?"

Charlotte watched for a moment and then said, "Nope."

"Good, then we can start our turn. Ask us if we are ready to tack."

"Okay. Ready to tack?" Charlotte watched as Tim freed the sheet from his winch while Aunt Alice wrapped the sheet around hers. She held on to it.

"Ready," said Tim and Alice together. "Now say, tacking."

"Tacking," said Charlotte.

"Now turn the boat toward that point you saw over your right shoulder."

Charlotte turned the wheel, focusing on the white boat until it was in front of her. There was a piece of black tape wrapped around the wheel to mark where it was centered. She centered the wheel and corrected a little to the left and to the right a couple of times, to maintain the white boat right in front of her.

In the meantime, Tim managed the jib sail. It had moved from being filled with air on the left side to being filled on the right side. He double checked that Aunt Alice had secured her sheet. They barely lost any forward momentum, and Aunt Alice and Tim cheered.

"Well done team."

Charlotte breathed a deep breath and easily let it go. She felt better than earlier that morning.

"Okay, now I want to handle a sheet. Someone take back the helm please." Tim stepped up and gave her a hug before she left the helm. This was the first time a handsome man had hugged her. She felt her cheeks warm, and her insides melt, just a bit. It felt so good.

Aunt Alice looked at her watch again. "Let's head in. It's going to be dark in a couple of hours."

They chatted happily until the boat was about to turn into the inlet. Tim turned the boat into the wind and started the motor but kept it in neutral. "Charlotte, come take the helm. Alice and I will tuck the sails away."

Charlotte took the helm, happily repeating what she had done not that long ago. She held on to the big wheel while Tim stood on the deck ready to guide the sails as they each came down. Aunt Alice unclamped halyards to control their descent. First the jib. Once it was down Tim rolled it over on itself and tucked it out the side of the deck and then stepped up to the boom to handle the main sail. Aunt Alice lifted the halyard out of the clamps and let it slide through her hands while Tim flipped the mainsail back and forth, layering it over the boom.

Just before the main was halfway down, Charlotte's knee accidentally knocked the motor into gear. Tim leapt from the deck to help Aunt Alice with the halyard which was being tugged by the wind. He told Charlotte to put the boat into neutral and to get it back in irons. She managed to put the engine in neutral but not knowing what in irons was, and hoping she was doing the right thing, she turned the wheel. That seemed to make things worse.

"Turn the wheel the other way, and a little slower. Head for that dock." Tim pointed to a white dock across the water on the shore.

Charlotte turned slowly, but too far, and found that they were moving too fast in the other direction. Before she knew it, Tim was beside her, getting the boat back on course.

"Sorry."

"Not to worry. Nobody got hurt," he said and then reminded her what direction to steer the boat.

"What's in irons?"

"A boat is in irons when it points straight into the wind. There is no wind in the sails and the boat stops moving. We get the sails down easily when it is in irons. With the engine running but in neutral we can have quick control and move- ment if we need to while we put down the sails." Tim returned to the deck after asking Aunt Alice if she was okay.

Charlotte looked at her aunt who seemed quite content sitting in the cockpit.

"I'm fine Tim. Thanks for your recovery."

Tim made short work of taking down the rest of the mainsail and then grabbed the fenders and lines he had put into the salon earlier that day. He tied the fenders back in place and attached the lines to the boat at the points where it was tied to the dock.

"Thanks Tim. Now Charlotte, you sit tight, and Tim will get us to the dock."

"Are you all right, Aunt Alice? You didn't get hurt with my steering?"

"No Charlotte, I'm okay. The boat was going too slow to have hurt anyone. It was just surprising." Aunt Alice smiled at Charlotte with warmth in her eyes. She bent over and patted Charlotte on the knee.

Charlotte sat still until the boat was nearing the dock. "Do you want me to do anything, Tim?" she offered.

"No, I've got it." He slowed the boat as they neared the dock, put it into neutral and let it glide slowly to the dock. He grabbed the line on the stern and tied it to the dock. He then hurried to the front of the boat to tie that the line to the dock.

"There we go. I can only do that without the motor on because this bay is so protected and there are no waves," he said and smiled at Charlotte and Alice.

"And because you have done it a thousand times. Thanks so much Tim." Alice smiled her appreciation.

They were a quiet group as they finished tucking everything away, secured the boat to the dock, and walked to the cars at the rescue center.

"Thanks Alice and Charlotte. That was fun. Next Sunday Alice? And Charlotte, will you join us again?"

"No, I won't. I'm going home on Friday."

"Too bad. Well, lovely to meet you again, Charlotte. Alice, I'll talk to you during the week." Tim climbed into his Jeep and drove away.

Charlotte and her aunt climbed into her Jetta and made their way back to her aunt's house. At first, they were quiet as Aunt Alice drove along the windy, narrow road that led away from the center. Her rock music playlist played softly in the background.

"Do you want to talk about it?" Aunt Alice's voice was quiet but kind.

"Another failure."

"But you tried."

"And I failed. I'm not cut out for new things."

"Don't be so hard on yourself. First times suck. You'll be better the next time."

Aunt Alice left Charlotte in her own thoughts and hummed to the music until they parked at the apartment. They got out of the car together and walked to the main door. Irene stepped off the side of the stoop of the apartment.

"Hello Charlotte. Hello Alice. What have you been doing while I have been sitting here waiting for you?" Irene's toned implied she had been waiting a long time.

Charlotte forgot the events of the day. Finding her mother at the apartment wasn't anything she had expected. Suddenly dogs and boats weren't that important.

nineteen

. . .

"CHARLOTTE, what have you done with your hair? I see your aunt is having an influence on you. And Alice. Nice to see you again. I trust you and Charlotte have enjoyed - what did you call it - reconnecting. What has she said about me?"

"Nothing Mother. We've not talked about you." Charlotte lied. She felt defensive, worried that her mother would find out she was having a good time with Aunt Alice.

Aunt Alice stepped up to the apartment door. "We are just back from sailing, Irene. Come on in. Let's put on some tea."

———

"I can't believe that you two have spent all this time together and haven't spoken about me at all." Irene was toying with her teacup at the kitchen table where they all sat. No one was really drinking or eating the cookies.

"Irene, what do you mean?"

There was silence. Charlotte looked from her aunt to her mother as if waiting for someone in a gunfight to draw.

"Oh, I guess I was just missing Charlotte, and, since I have never been to this house or the center I thought, what the heck."

"That's pretty brave of you, Mother. You have never been out of Beckerville."

"Oh, I came to the island once, a long time ago."

"But not to my house."

"No, not to this house."

"Why haven't you ever visited me here, Irene?"

Charlotte felt like they each laid down a gauntlet. It was curious that Aunt Alice was eyeing Irene so directly, as if trying to see inside her. Charlotte felt things needed to be said between the two of them that she didn't need to hear. A walk would do her good.

"I'm going to leave you two to catch up. I'll take a walk on the beach." Neither woman seemed to notice her slip away, and for that she was grateful. They might have come with her and brought that unsettling energy with them.

Charlotte deeply breathed in the ocean air as she walked. She went over the events of the day, remembering how scared she was that Fred and Barney were fighting, and the helplessness of not being able to make them stop. She didn't like feeling uncomfortable, or like she had no control over what was happening to her. The logic of doing accounting, the practices, and rules were defined and well understood. She felt safe in that world. This goes here, that goes there. And things balanced, or you figured out why. You got them to balance. Sometimes there were surprises in the end, but often you could see the story build as you put the records together. Life outside of accounting practices, life in an office, life with her mother, even life here on the island wasn't like that at all. Things happened. Uncomfortable things. Sometimes you felt like you could manage. She laughed. Before they let her go from work, she had little control over what happened to her. Now she had all the control she wanted. If she used it.

Charlotte stopped in her tracks on the beach. She wrapped

her sweater around her and hugged it to herself. If she was going to change her life, uncomfortable things had to happen. She had to decide how uncomfortable she was willing to be. She wasn't sure she knew that answer.

After an hour of walking, she decided it might be safe to return to her aunt's apartment. She found the two women on the deck sipping a glass of her aunt's favorite wine.

"Charlotte, did you have a pleasant walk?" Irene asked.

"I did. Thanks." Charlotte looked at her unusually serene mother.

"Did you two get things sorted out?"

"What? Nothing needed sorting. What a strange thing to say. What were you thinking, Charlotte?" Irene said.

Charlotte felt silly and stood silent, looking out at the ocean, wishing the tears not to fall. Aunt Alice rose and smiled gently at Charlotte. She gave her arm a gentle squeeze.

"How long are you here for Irene?"

Charlotte was glad Aunt Alice asked what she too wanted to know.

"Oh, I thought I'd stay until Charlotte's visit is over. That way we can drive back together." Charlotte thought Irene looked smug with her reply.

Both Alice and Irene looked at Charlotte. She hoped her face didn't show how much she didn't want that to happen.

"She has to get home to look for a job, don't you Charlotte?"

This time Charlotte felt Irene's eyes on her face, daring her to deny that fact.

"Why don't the three of us go out for supper? I'll take us to one of my favorite Italian places. It's not dressy but we need to shower, don't we Charlotte?" Charlotte and her aunt disappeared into their respective rooms leaving Irene alone. Charlotte was first to be ready.

"Mother, why are you here?"

"You're not glad to see me?"

"I see you every day. Why are you here?"

"I've not been to the island in a very long time. Besides Alice did invite me too."

Aunt Alice entered the room. "I did. I just wonder why you didn't come with Charlotte. What made you change your mind?"

"You wanted to reconnect, so I thought I should be part of that. We are the only family we have."

Charlotte felt that fact sit heavy in the room.

twenty

. . .

"COME ON, LET'S GO EAT." Aunt Alice grabbed her keys and led the women out of the apartment. The drive was quiet. Aunt Alice parked the car and escorted them down a side street. Midway down that street hung a sign over a door that said *Spagucci's*. They stood in the vestibule to wait their turn. The walls were decorated with paintings of wine glasses, grapes, leaves and plates of delicious looking food. The seating was basic, wooden chairs and tables. Soothing music played overhead. The bay window at the front let in enough light to brighten the whole restaurant and the buzz of voices added to the feeling of happiness that everything imbued. Charlotte smiled. This was the kind of place she expected Aunt Alice to like. She noted the tables were tight together, and the place was full. *Good, the closeness of the tables won't allow for personal conversations*, Charlotte thought, with relief.

They were seated and handed menus which offered many pasta options plus a variety of salads. Watching plates go by her as they reviewed the menu, Charlotte's stomach rumbled in anticipation.

"I found this restaurant when I first came to the island. It was inexpensive, so I took myself out for supper once a week." Aunt Alice said.

"Do you dine out often?"

Charlotte didn't like the sound of Irene's voice.

"No, but I decided when I started working that I could afford to take myself out once a week. I have stuck with that." Aunt Alice stood up as she finished speaking. "Angelo, how are you?" She hugged and kissed a dark-haired man who arrived at their table. He hugged and kissed her back.

"I am well Alice. How are you? I wasn't expecting you until Monday." He looked at the ladies at the table as if they could provide the explanation.

"I had unexpected company and there is only one place to bring company. This is my sister Irene and my niece Charlotte."

He extended his arms to both women who rose to accept his greeting. It surprised Charlotte that a stranger would hug and kiss her on the check. But she noticed her mother was petrified. Angelo didn't look like he noticed.

"So good to have family visit. Welcome. Is this your first time to Victoria?"

"It is," Alice answered for them.

"It must be, otherwise I would have met them before." He winked at Aunt Alice.

Aunt Alice laughed. "Of course. You and the family are well?"

"They are. We are just helping my brother Dino out. You know he has his pub up the island."

"Of course. Tim and I sail there at least once a month."

"His wife had twins, so their hands are full. But they are so happy."

"Please give him my congratulations. Tim and I will be that way in a couple of weeks. So good to see you, as always."

"We will see you next week. A pleasure to meet you Charlotte and Irene. Hope you enjoy your visit to the island. Maybe we will see you again?"

Aunt Alice sat down and smiled at her guests. "I met Angelo my first visit here. He was a waiter for his father then. He has since taken over the restaurant and he and his family run it. They make the best pasta in town."

"You two looked pretty close." Again, that tone.

"Mother," Charlotte hissed.

"Do you have no friends Irene?"

Irene's face stilled to rock. Charlotte noticed a blush. She knew her mother had only Charlotte in her life.

"Angelo and I have been friends forever. He is a good man, a loving husband and father. We help each other out, me with his accounting and he with my sailing. But we are just friends."

Irene opened her mouth and surprised Charlotte when she closed it and sipped her water.

"And Tim is my veterinarian and sailing partner." Aunt Alice eyes seem to challenge Irene to say anything about that.

Charlotte hurried to change the subject. "What other favorite places do you have on the island, Aunt Alice?"

Grateful the mood lightened, Charlotte happily tucked into the chicken parmigiana. Aunt Alice entertained them with the stories of her adventures exploring the island over the years. She talked about the coves she'd found where she could read and swim without crowds. She described a few of the kitschy stores in the small towns that sold local artwork. She giggled as she told them of the goats that lived on the roof of a building up the island. Goats on a house roof seemed so ridiculous in her aunt's description that they laughed. Charlotte was relieved when she heard Irene chuckle. Charlotte hadn't been sure if Irene was enjoying herself, she had been so uncharacteristically quiet since the food arrived.

When the check came, Irene reached for her purse.

"Irene, you don't have to buy," Aunt Alice said.

"But I interrupted your visit. It's the least I can do for putting up with me." Irene walked to the till and initiated the transaction with the cashier. When Charlotte and Alice joined her, Irene seemed upset. "Apparently your Angelo has paid for our meal."

Charlotte watched Aunt Alice search the restaurant for Angelo. When she spotted him, she mouthed *thank you.* He merely blew her a kiss.

"Well, that's that then. Try to do something nice and look what happens." Irene opened the door and left the restaurant. The atmosphere in the car was quiet again.

At the apartment Charlotte gathered her things from the bedroom and tucked them into the living room. "You can sleep in the spare bedroom, Mother. I'll sleep on the couch."

Irene opened her mouth to argue, looked at the bedroom door, entered, and shut the bedroom door behind her.

Charlotte sagged and fell into the cozy living room chair. "Wow, that was hard," she muttered.

"We'll get there, my dear. Don't worry." Aunt Alice patted her on the shoulder.

"It just wrecks everything. I was having so much fun."

"We'll just continue doing what we were doing. It will be fine. I'm glad you are enjoying yourself. Me too." They moved to the deck with a glass of wine in their hands to watch the evening turn into night.

Neither noticed Irene move to the kitchen and pour herself a glass of water and stare at them sharing the deck and the wine. She grimaced and returned to her room, shutting the door.

———

The next morning, over a quiet breakfast, Irene asked, "Do you think I could see the center today?"

"Why don't we do that after breakfast?" suggested Aunt Alice.

Charlotte was grateful for the idea. It would mean they didn't have to sit around looking at each other all day. She was last to use the washroom and was surprised to find the apartment empty when she got out of the shower.

Aunt Alice and her mother were in the car when Charlotte got to the parking lot. She could see they were in a heated conversation and could hear the anger in their voices through the open windows. She stopped far enough away to hear them, but out of sight.

"I just don't think you had to be so unkind. She was so delighted with how she looked with the new hair and clothes. You took the joy right out of it with your comments." Aunt Alice's voice was not like she had ever heard before.

"Well, I was just so surprised. She always dresses conservatively." Irene was her usual cagey self.

"So plain you mean."

"Well, she's not a pretty girl, let's not try to make something out of nothing."

"Irene. How can you be so cruel? You are a bully, just like Momma. You don't have a pleasant thing to say about anyone or anything."

"I am not like Momma. How can you say that?"

"I've watched you push and poke at that child since you arrived. You are lucky she is composed of tough stuff. What happened to Charlotte wasn't her fault. And you make it out like it is by how you treat her."

Charlotte thought she better not linger any longer and walked toward the car. The women looked at each other, and Charlotte thought they had given each other a signal that this wasn't the time to finish the argument.

"Listen Charlotte, I'd like to take Irene for a drive before we go to the center. There are some things we need to talk about." Aunt Alice put the car into reverse and Charlotte watched them leave the parking lot. *I wonder what wasn't my fault?* She returned to the apartment.

twenty-one

· · ·

IN THE CAR, the silence was dark and cold. Alice spoke first. "You just about let the cat out of the bag. We agreed."

"Alice it's time she knew."

"I said she wouldn't know until I passed. You promised you would keep that secret."

"I know. But this is hard now, with us seeing each other. She deserves to know the truth."

"She is only seeing us together because you surprised us. What is this about, Irene?"

"Well, I ..." Irene chewed on her lip, as if deciding what to say.

"You wanted to make sure I wasn't telling her things about you."

"I did not. I thought it was time she knew the truth. She deserves that from us both." Irene sounded convinced that was a good reason for her unplanned visit.

"She deserves to be loved, unconditionally by both of us. It wasn't her fault I got pregnant, Pete died, and Momma foisted her on you. It wasn't her fault that you had to raise her. I could have raised her, but Momma interfered."

"I always wondered why she did that. Do you know? It wasn't about you not being able to raise her."

"She was trying to make it up to you." Alice looked at Irene as she said that and then pivoted her attention to driving.

"Make what up to me?" Out of the corner of her eye, Alice noticed the surprise on Irene's face.

"Don't you know? She didn't let you get a job when we were teenagers. She tore up your cooking school acceptance letter and made you think you weren't accepted."

"What?"

"The letter was in the garbage. I found it and wanted to tell you so many times, but Momma was such a bear that I figured if I did, she would throw a fit. I hoped another letter would come to tell you, but I guess Momma threw those away, too."

"I got accepted into cooking school?"

"You did. How come you didn't pursue that?"

"I didn't know I was accepted. All I knew was I couldn't wait to get out of that house. When Jim proposed, I could get away from Momma and so I accepted and left."

"You didn't get that far away. Jim's farm was only down the road."

"But at least not in the same yard."

"You do know she bought that property between yours and the farm so that you could be neighbors."

"She didn't."

"She did. She made Jim promise not to tell you she had bought it for you, so you didn't feel beholden to her."

"How do you know all this?"

"Daddy."

"Oh, right. You and Daddy and your clandestine phone calls. What else do you know that I don't?"

"I think she took Charlotte from me and gave her to you because you and Jim weren't able to have children. And she was sure I would be an unfit mother. She worried they would take Charlotte away because I was unmarried. In her mind, single women could not raise children. At least not as well as a husband and wife."

"You would not have neglected Charlotte."

"No, I wouldn't have. But you know Mother, she was in Victoria and had Charlotte in the car back to Beckerville before I could barely get out of bed."

"You couldn't stop Momma." Irene agreed.

"Our mother? Not a chance. When I was a little girl, I challenged Momma about something. I don't remember what it was now, but she came back at me with such a roar and snarl that I ran outside and hid in the barn. She scared me to death. I wasn't sure what I had done to make her so mad, but I knew never to cross her again. Until I could escape to university, I knew I had to keep away from her to survive."

There was silence in the car as Alice continued driving the shoreline road.

"I do love Charlotte, you know."

"It doesn't show. That woman, she's not a girl now, came here looking like a lost lamb searching for someone to love her. And she is easy to love. You and Jim did a good job raising her, but I'm not sure you did a good job loving her."

"How can you love someone that is not really yours? That could be taken away in a heartbeat?" Irene pleaded.

"Oh Irene. She was always yours. I couldn't have her, and after you told me to stay away, I had to let her go. I'm not sure I have forgiven you for that yet, but I try a little harder every day."

"Well, it must be satisfying to have her here."

"It is."

"You'll let her come back?"

Alice's head turned to see tears dripping down her sister's face. "Charlotte will decide what she wants to do. We must both accept that."

"And we still will keep the secret?"

"And we will still keep the secret. Until I am gone."

"Have it your way then."

———

Charlotte sensed a peace between the sisters that hadn't been there before when they returned. She was relieved. It would be a long week if the energy between them remained hostile. On the way to the center, Aunt Alice played her usual playlist and even sang a little. Charlotte joined in quietly and Irene looked out the window.

Only Bonnie was at the center when they arrived. She was cleaning pens and feeding the dogs. Aunt Alice showed Irene the full facility with the same pleasure as when she had showed Charlotte around.

Irene surprised Charlotte by her interest. "This is special, Alice. You've done something good here."

Charlotte was as surprised with the compliment as her aunt's raised eyebrows showed.

"Thanks Irene. I like to think we matter. That this matters."

"The dog next door to us in Beckerville is treated so badly. And because he is, he always snarls and yaps at Charlotte when she walks by. He would love kindness."

Charlotte's head almost swiveled off her neck. She didn't think Irene knew the dog next door was so aggressive.

"He makes you even more afraid of dogs, doesn't he Charlotte? Has she told you about her fear of dogs, Alice? You should ask her about it."

Aunt Alice wrapped her arm around Charlotte's shoulder as they followed Irene in what became her own self-guided tour. "We've solved that I think," said Aunt Alice.

Irene stopped and looked at Alice and Charlotte. But said nothing. As she walked by the pens each of the dogs barked loudly and then stopped barking and wagged their tales as Aunt Alice and Charlotte followed. Charlotte looked at her aunt and they smiled in conspiracy with the dogs.

"She naturally creates tension, doesn't she?" Aunt Alice whispered in Charlotte's ear. "No wonder you came here."

Charlotte smiled. There was nothing to say.

Irene came to the fork in the path that led to the dock or back to the center. "Where does this go?"

"Oh, it's just a loop that we walk the dogs on. Why don't we go back into the city and have an early supper on my deck? We can plan something for the evening."

Their route back to the car took them by Larry's favorite spot on the deck at the back of the house. He was on his usual pillow and seemed asleep, but he stood up when Irene was about five steps from him. He barked his not so fierce *woof* twice at her and then settled back down when Aunt Alice approached him and scratched his face.

Charlotte smiled. *Even dogs know when someone is not kind-hearted.* She felt her conflicted feelings about her mother were vindicated by all the dogs' reactions to Irene. She knew she should love her mother. After all, parents give up so much to raise a child. But shouldn't they give something back, like the gifts of love and kindness? Irene was always cool and aloof. And her mouth could be vicious. Not qualities that made you feel like you were loved. Charlotte mulled over that on the drive back to the apartment.

———

Irene took her tea to the deck while Charlotte helped her aunt prepare supper. Alice turned on her rock playlist and gathered items from the fridge. As she put things on the island, she explained to Charlotte what she intended to make for the meal.

When one of their favorite songs played, Charlotte felt her

aunt pull her hand to join in a dance to the music. The heaviness of the morning lifted in Charlotte, and she danced and giggled in the kitchen with her aunt. Charlotte couldn't remember this kind of joy with her mother and a choked sob consumed her. She gasped and snorted and then started to cry a full body sob.

"Charlotte what is it?" Aunt Alice immediately stopped dancing.

"Oh, Aunt Alice. I've never felt this way before. So light and happy. So alive and loved."

"Oh, my dear. I'm so sorry it has taken this long to feel that way. Now that you know what it feels like, you need to make choices that sustain it." She gathered Charlotte into her arms and Charlotte felt herself cuddled in tight.

As her head was stroked in the caress, Charlotte let the long-bottled emotions run through and then out of her body. Charlotte didn't hear the deck door open and Irene step back into the apartment.

"Well, isn't this cozy? I guess the circle has been closed back up, hasn't it Alice. I see I'm not wanted." And she marched to her room and slammed the door.

Charlotte took a step out of her aunt's arms; torn between their comfort and the need to convince her mother she was needed. But in her heart, Charlotte knew that would be lying. The only person she needed was Aunt Alice.

Charlotte felt Aunt Alice look into her very soul.

"Are you okay now?"

Charlotte merely nodded. She could feel the Irene tornado unleashing fury in the bedroom and wanted to escape.

"You stay here, I'll go see what Irene's upset about." Alice closed the bedroom door behind her, and Charlotte's heard muffled voices and the odd word yelled. She couldn't catch the gist of the conversation and toyed with walking to the door to listen closer. Worried she might hear something she didn't want to know; she chose the deck instead and closed its door behind her so she could shut out what was going on in the apartment. She heard a loud bang and turned to watch the two women carry on a conversation in the kitchen. She opened the door a bit.

"It's clear I'm not wanted here," Irene repeated.

"Of course, we want you here Irene. It is lovely having us together. We are family."

"Well, my daughter and you have resumed that special friendship that you had when she was younger. I didn't like it then and I don't like it now. Except now I can't stop it."

Charlotte watched her mother's fists clench and unclench. She recognized it as one of her signs of distress.

"I was hoping that it would be different now that Charlotte is older. I hoped she would come here and not see you as Alice the Great. But I can see that you have turned her against me."

"Irene, you are being ridiculous."

"Ridiculous? Me, ridiculous? You are the one who left us. Who got yourself into a mess that Momma had to rescue you from and then it became my burden to bear? And now, after all the work I have done, all the sacrifices I made, I see you and Charlotte hugging. Like you love her. Like a …"

"Like an aunt should love her niece. And if you could open your heart and mind a little, you could love her like that too."

"It's too late for me."

"It's never too late to show love, Irene."

"Oh, Alice, you always were such a Pollyanna. So disillusioned, so innocent. No wonder you got …" Irene broke off as she noticed Charlotte moving toward the island.

"Charlotte, I am going home. I've had enough of being here with you two. You enjoy your holiday, but I expect you to be back soon to get a job. I won't be able to pick you up at the airport. You'll have to make other arrangements." And, in her usual abrupt fashion, Irene picked up her bag, opened the apartment door and swished out, slamming the door.

It was like a vacuum had been created by her exit. And then the vacuum disappeared, and the energy flew out the deck doors and was gone. It was replaced by the rock playlist and the salt smell and happy bird noises of life by the ocean. Charlotte stood still, trying to replay the words her mother had just said.

"That was a surprise for Mother to visit you here," said Aunt Alice.

"I'm not sure why she came," Charlotte said.

"She is still needy. She needs to feel like she is loved. Momma only made her feel inadequate as a wife and mother."

"That's what caused her to be so angry and mean? She didn't think she could measure up?"

"I think so. Momma's expectations were so high. Too high. Your mother got caught up in that. And I think she didn't have anywhere to turn. Any other support."

"What about my dad?"

"Your father did what he could to make her happy, but I don't think anything could overcome the influence of Momma."

"But what about you? Did Gramma do that to you too?"

"Oh, I knew I would never measure up, so I never even tried. I wanted joy and happiness in my life. It always felt so heavy and serious around Momma. Thank goodness for my dad. He was fun. He knew I would not stay in Beckerville, that I would have a career and leave Beckerville, eventually. He was okay with that."

"Was that hard to do?"

"What? Leave Beckerville? No, it wasn't hard. I was scared, but more scared of what I would become if I stayed there."

Charlotte sat in silence.

"Still thinking of leaving Beckerville? And maybe coming to the island?"

"I don't know. It's a big move. I'm not sure I belong here, though. I am crap with the dogs, and I can't sail well. There must be a life for me somewhere."

"You belong where you feel loved and worthy. Where you matter. And you matter to me. Besides, there is a job for you here if you want it."

twenty-two

. . .

CHARLOTTE SHARED the events of Irene's visit with Janine later that day on an online chat.

"I can't believe your mother actually drove to see you," said Janine. "I don't think she has ever left Beckerville. Has she?"

"She came to the island once, but I don't know when. That surprised the heck out of me, I didn't know she went anywhere."

"What did she want?"

"I feel like she was checking up on me. Checking if I was having a good time with Aunt Alice. The two of them got into a conversation that was clearly not something I should hear and so I went for a walk."

"What were they talking about?"

"I don't know, but they seemed more peaceful when I got back. I was thankful for that. Then it started all over again the next morning. Something about it not being my fault."

"What's not your fault?"

"I don't know. I'll ask Aunt Alice when it's right."

"Wow. That's all I can say. How's the dog thing going?"

"Oh, not so good. I took two for a walk a couple of days

ago and they started playing, although it looked like fighting to me and I couldn't stop them. I didn't know what to do. Sandy had to come and rescue me."

"Are you okay?"

"Oh, yeah. Just my pride. I can't do anything well, except sit in an office and do paperwork. How exciting is that? Did I tell you my aunt offered me a job?"

"Really? Did you say yes?"

"What? No. I couldn't move here. I don't belong here. My home is Beckerville. I was born and raised there. Besides, the dogs don't like me, and I am a clumsy sailor. I'm not my aunt. I'm not brave enough to give up everything I've ever known and go somewhere I've never been and do things I've never done before. I'm better off finding a quiet little accounting job in Beckerville and resuming my life there."

"What do you mean, clumsy sailor?"

"Aunt Alice, Tim, and I went sailing. It was lovely. The ocean breezes are so soothing. I feel like I am home on the water."

"And you still didn't accept the job offer."

"Oh, Aunt Alice wasn't serious. I think she thought I did such a good job that I should keep on doing it. She will find someone here."

"So, you are definitely returning to Beckerville."

"Yup. Two more days. Will you pick me up? Mother has made it clear she won't be able to."

"Of course. Oh, wait. Who is Tim?"

"He's the vet they use at the rescue center."

"Is he cute?"

"Oh, Janine." Charlotte felt relief at the change of topic. "Yes, he is good looking. He's a marvelous sailor, knows what to do when things go wrong and is calm about making it right. He's a friendly man."

"What went wrong?"

"Oh, I lost focus, forgot my job and the boat started moving when they were putting down the sails."

"Then what happened?"

"Tim just told me what to do. After he put the sails down, he explained what went wrong."

"Where was your aunt during this?"

"She was sitting on the boat, just watching." Charlotte realized her aunt did nothing during this time. Her forehead creased in puzzlement.

"What is it?"

"My aunt did nothing."

"Was she hurt or jarred?"

"No, she said she was fine. I asked her. She just sat there, like she was exhausted."

"Was Tim mad?"

"No, he was kind. Helpful. Treated me like a beginner."

"Of course, he did. You are a beginner. First times suck. They are there to test your resolve to try something new."

"Yeah, yeah." Charlotte chuckled again. "You know, I could actually see myself living here, working at the center, sailing with my aunt. Getting to know her better. She is lovely. I am so glad she asked me to come for a visit."

"And that you went. But you declined her job offer."

"I did. I'd best go. My flight arrives at two o'clock, see you then."

"You bet. Enjoy yourself. Walk dogs and go sailing again if you get a chance."

Fat chance I'll do that, thought Charlotte as she hung up the phone.

Charlotte sat down at the table where a chicken casserole with mushrooms and herbs was served with baby potatoes and a broccoli salad. "Yum. This looks delicious. Thank you. And thank you for inviting me here. I have really enjoyed my time with you."

"Me too. You are sure you won't take me up on my offer of a job?"

"No. I belong in Beckerville and my mom needs me."

"No, she doesn't Charlotte. She needs someone to bully. That doesn't have to be you. A life is meant to be lived. You should feel complete from living your life, not empty because you have endured it."

Silence sat at the table with the women and didn't move. Tears fell from Charlotte's eyes. She didn't feel them coming; they were suddenly there, pouring down her face. "I don't think I can leave my mother. She will be so upset. I promised Dad and I won't break my promise to him."

"She will be upset. You are right. But is it your choice or hers?"

Alice reached for the tissue box on the counter and pushed it toward Charlotte. "You have been through a lot with your mom. Irene is unhappy and is making you the same way. She can't bear to see you happy because it means she has no control over you. Irene is the one who must change, and nothing frightens Irene more than change."

"How do you know?"

"Because I grew up with her. There was always change at our house. Momma changed the furniture, the wallpaper, the paint every year, claiming the house needed to be freshened up. Our dad would roll his eyes and go back to the cows and fields. Irene and I always had to help. I just did the work, but you could see it unsettled Irene. Like the ground under her was always shifting. Momma was the same with the garden. No plants grew in the same place two years in a row, and she tried different vegetables all the time. Stuff we had never heard of, stuff we would never eat. Nothing stayed the same. All that effort because she wasn't happy. It was exhausting. Irene is like her a lot. Change frightens your mother. You aren't the same as her."

"How can you be so sure?" Charlotte sniffled and wiped her tears away.

"You came here to see me. And I think you are a cheerful person, like your dad. You seem to have the happy gene that ran on his side. For that I am grateful."

Silence sat at the table again, but this time, a contemplative one, while they finished their supper.

"Come on. Let's go for a walk on the beach and find some ice cream."

They spent the rest of the evening enjoying the early summer wind and the smell of the water. Birds flew in the ocean breezes, catching an updraft and resting on it before flapping to find another one.

Charlotte felt the calm return to her. The calm that was unsettled by her mother. *Did she have the strength to cut away and live her own life?*

twenty-three

. . .

THE LAST DAYS in Victoria flew by. The time spent at the apartment, on the deck, watching the ocean, Charlotte wanted to last forever. She would cherish the view of the great grey water and the mountains and this blue sky. She closed her eyes absorbing the sounds of the birds, the people chatting as they walked, and the smells of the salt water that it offered. She promised to resurrect those memories when she needed solace back in Beckerville.

At the rescue center, the days flew too. She was busy keeping the accounts current and writing procedures so the next bookkeeper would have some resources. It was curious no one had been interviewed yet. She decided to ask her aunt about the plans for her replacement. "Do you want my help with the interviews?" Every day Charlotte watched her aunt manage all the areas of the rescue center. She thought that doing the interviews for her would take something off her plate.

"Oh, dear. I forgot all about that." Aunt Alice's face pressed into a frown. "You are sure you won't come to work for us here?"

"I am sure. Sorry, but I think I belong back in Beckerville. Not here."

"You don't look sure."

"Aunt Alice, I think I was lucky to come here, to see a different life. But I'm not sure anyone gets it all."

"Sounds like something your mother would say."

Charlotte thought about it for a minute. She had heard her mother say that to her. Often. "I guess so. But it is true."

"I have it all here, but I hope you figure out where you need to be and soon." Aunt Alice gave her a hug and said, "Don't worry about the interviews. We'll find someone."

Charlotte watched as she walked away. In her mind, she admitted she wanted it all, like Aunt Alice had, though it felt as if she never had that chance. *Was now the chance? Would a new job in Beckerville give her new options and get her closer to having it all?*

She picked Lucy's leash off the rack, intending to take her for a slow amble down the path. Lucy had grown used to Charlotte's advances and easily let Charlotte rub her face and her back. Her eyes looked brighter. She wagged her tail when she spied Charlotte coming toward her. Charlotte opened the gate to Lucy's pen and kept a foot out ahead of her to keep the puppies from escaping. They were round little balls of fur. Their noses were close to the ground as they explored everything they could smell. Charlotte bent to pick up one of the most adventurous ones who was trying to slip by her foot. The others weren't so curious, and she was able to keep them in the pen with her foot and the gate. "Come on, little one. You aren't quite ready for the big world." She placed him with his brothers.

She shut the gate behind her and slid a toy to distract the puppies while she put the leash on their mother. Lucy rose and slowly walked behind Charlotte to the gate. Lucy quickly exited the pen, leaving the puppies engrossed with the stuffed bird. Lucy seemed to pick up her pace as they headed to the fields. *She must be ready for a break from puppies.*

"Care for some company?"

Charlotte turned, surprised to see Tim there. She didn't know he was coming today.

"Sure. If you have the time."

"Oh, a brief walk will not put me off schedule too much." Tim turned toward the path along the fence. "How are you doing?"

"I'm okay. I go home tomorrow."

"I know. Your aunt told me. Too bad. She could really use some help. She said she offered you a job."

"She did, although I don't think it was a genuine offer." She noticed Tim raise an eyebrow. "I think she was being nice because I got everything caught up."

"I've known your aunt for a very long time, and I've never seen her do things just to be nice. She is always very serious. Especially about business. And this center. You may want to reconsider."

"But I have a life in Beckerville. And my mother needs my help." Even to her ears her excuses sounded weak.

"Well, I'm not sure how you leave all this. Warmer winters than you have inland, the ocean, these dogs, an aunt who loves you."

Charlotte looked at him under a creased forehead.

"I know you haven't known each other for very long, but she loves you. And I think she needs you too." Tim said.

"How do you decide?"

Tim smiled. "I thought you had decided already?"

Charlotte grinned. "I can't deny this is a wonderful place. The dogs, the people, the sailing. Even when I am terrible at things, I am happy."

"Does that sound like the right choice, then?" The chattering birds in the field and the whispering wind in the trees filled in the silence between the two. "Lucy is doing well."

Charlotte was grateful Tim changed the subject. "She is. Although those puppies keep her busy."

"That's the nature of puppies. It won't be long before they go to new homes. Lucy will soon be alone again."

"Won't she miss her puppies?"

"You know, I don't know. I've seen dogs meet each other after being separated and you can see they sort of remember each other. I don't know if dogs pine after each other like people can do, though."

"Not the same connection I guess."

"I think people's relationships are nuanced with words and actions that are remembered but rarely well understood. At least with a dog, you know where you stand. They are rarely mean, and when they are, they have an excellent reason for it. It's not easy to be sure why a human being is mean."

Charlotte studied Tim's face. "Why do you say that?"

"Oh, I've had some rough relationships in my time. That's why I enjoy being a vet so much. Especially with dogs. Usually, the solution is uncomplicated. I almost always get a tail wag even after I've had to freeze them to take out a porcupine quill or fix a broken bone. What do you like about accounting?"

"Oh, things almost always add up. There are checks and balances to make sure it is right. There is a story in the numbers that helps you decide where the business needs improvement. It's solitary work I enjoy."

Charlotte peered out of the corner of her eye, gauging Tim's reaction.

"Like without help? Or alone?"

"Both, I think. It's just me and the paper and the numbers. We understand each other."

"With dogs you have to spend the time to understand and communicate with them."

"That is different for sure."

"But you and Lucy have become quite comfortable with each other."

"We have. She is a lovely dog."

"So, worth the time?"

"Yes."

The bird chirps and the wind whispers filled the silence again. Charlotte tried to think of something else to talk about. She wanted to run back to the center because Tim's words were making her uncomfortable. She had so many things running through her mind that conflicted with what she was telling herself. The fork in the path that took them to the dock was ahead.

"Care to take a last look at the sailboat?"

"Sure, why not?"

"I always wanted to sail," Tim said. "When your aunt offered to take me out it was like having a lifelong dream come true."

"When was the first time?"

"About a year ago."

"But you look so comfortable with it. You know all the words and you didn't get rattled when I lost my target on the shore."

"Patience is required when learning a new skill. Patience with yourself mostly. I've made my fair share of mistakes, too. One day the wind picked up when we were out. We were still in the bay, away from the inlet and very exposed. I was on the helm while Alice had gone below to grab lunch. I still don't know why, but I let go of the wheel. The boat heeled over hard."

"What is heeled over?"

"A sailboat leans away from the wind naturally. The boat stays upright because the weight of the keel balances the force of the wind on the sails. When there is no steering control on the rudder the boat turns in circles. Anyway, I heard a clunk downstairs and then your aunt asked me if I was on the helm."

Charlotte's eyes widened at his story.

"I had us straightened out by the time she came back up from below. She asked me what happened. I had to admit that I let go of the wheel. She told me that exact thing had happened to her once, when she was out with some friends. One of them was in the bathroom and almost landed with her head in the toilet."

They both chuckled.

"Anyway, she explained heeling and how that was the nature of boats. She made me stay on the helm and away we went."

"And you still sailed."

"To this day and many more. Will you ever sail again?"

"I don't know. I still feel bad not doing what I was told. I figure I am not meant to be a sailor."

"I think you are too hard on yourself. Nobody got hurt. And we recovered. You can't give up on things just because you have some rough bumps."

"Kind of like dogs and people."

"Exactly."

Charlotte stood on the hill looking down at the dock, taking in the water and boat. Feeling like she had no right to ask for this to be her life. No matter how badly she wanted it to be.

"We should head back. I have a few dogs to look at before my next appointment."

They walked back in companionable silence.

"Bye, Charlotte. Safe travels home." Tim gave her a hug.

People in Victoria give a lot of hugs, she thought.

twenty-four

. . .

AUNT ALICE WAS sorry she was going.

"I will miss you and am so glad you came. You have a place here any time. Remember. The job offer holds as well."

"Thank you, Aunt Alice." Charlotte hugged her back. Hard. "I'm not sure when, but I will visit again."

"Good. I was hoping you would say that. I love you, Charlotte." They looked at each other one more time before Charlotte walked down the long hallway to the departure gate seating area where she sat down heavily. She couldn't remember being told someone loved her since her dad's passing. She bent her head as she sat and let the tears fall. *Am I making a mistake? Should I stay here?* She wondered this for the tenth time that day.

Charlotte picked up her carry-on bag and stood up. She started walking back into the main area of the airport to find a cab and return to her aunt's house. Ten steps later, she stopped and walked back to where she had been sitting. She sat down and sighed.

By the time they announced the boarding call, Charlotte had no tears left, and she was clearer about what she was going to do. Still torn, but the plane was leaving.

———

The flight was quick, and she was soon enfolded Janine's hug at the end of the security gate and then arm in arm to get her bags from the carousel.

"Well, I think you look tortured."

Charlotte laughed. "I'm not sure if I should be here or in Victoria."

"Well, that makes it easy." Janine laughed back. "What are you going to do?"

"You are going to take me home. I am going to unpack, do laundry and have a long, hot bath. Mother will have a pile of job opportunities to look at. And I need to do an online search for apartment rentals."

"You sound sure about all that."

"I am. Forward steps. I have made my decision."

"Okay then. Let's get you home."

Charlotte sent a text to her aunt that she arrived home. And responded to her, *I'm glad,* with a heart emoji. She smiled when one returned.

There were several pages with job opportunities on Charlotte's table as she predicted. Her mother had been very busy. The rest of the suite looked the same, but it seemed dreary and dark. Not light and airy like her aunt's apartment. Charlotte put her bag down and sorted its contents for laundry. The mundane action helped her sort through her emotions. But she knew what her next step must be. With the load started, she scanned the pages.

Only two jobs interested Charlotte, so she completed their online applications. Her boss, Fuzziewig, had emailed her a reasonable reference letter. Although not filled with praise, what he had written was better than no reference at all. Online, she found a few apartments worth considering. She phoned to make appointments for viewing over the next two days.

———

None of the apartments appealed to her at all. They were too old and dated, or too small. It surprised Charlotte to find out how expensive they were. Without a job, she wasn't sure what she could afford. That would leave her in the basement suite for the future.

She wondered if buying a place was an option and spent some time looking at condos, townhouses, and mortgage calculators online. Those results were not any better than the rental market. Without a job, being approved for a mortgage presented another problem. That left her still in the basement suite.

For days, there were no requests for interviews, no better job opportunities, and no better apartments. Charlotte was pretty convinced she would live in the basement suite of her mother's house for the rest of her life. Facing a future of unemployment, she wondered about her aunt's job offer again when her cell phone rang.

A company requested she attend a job interview the next morning. With relief, Charlotte called Janine to go shopping for a new suit that afternoon. They planned a list of the better stores in Beckerville for business clothes. On the drive to them, Charlotte brought Janine up to date with her new home search.

"I've had little luck. The apartments are terrible. I never realized how lucky I was to live in the basement suite of my mother's house. It's not new, but it is in good shape."

"Paint and pillows can make anything look better. Don't overlook the potential in the apartments."

"Janine, I'm not sure there is potential in any of these."

"You need me to come with you the next time you look."

"I'm not sure I am looking any longer. No one will offer me a lease without a job."

"I suppose, but don't stop. Let's look at it again when you

have worked for a few weeks. Promise me you will take me with you."

"I promise. Now, let's look for a suit."

They spent the next couple of hours looking through racks of suits at a women's clothing store Charlotte had walked by many times but never entered. Janine was insistent they see what they offered. "Charlotte, this is an important interview. A new stylish suit will help you stand out from all the other applicants. You have good credentials and a good reference. Now you must look the part. Besides, that new hairdo deserves better clothes."

Charlotte tried on four different suits, two that she liked and two that Janine liked. Her choices were more conservative and understated than Janine's, they offered no real shaping and didn't flatter her figure. Janine's, however, suited Charlotte's curvy frame and long legs. One choice had a skirt, one had pants. After considering the many angles in the mirror, Charlotte had to admit that Janine's skirt suit was the best of the lot. Maybe it was the color. It was a teal green that flattered her tanned face.

Luckily, the suit needed no alterations, but it did need a new blouse. Janine escorted Charlotte to the little boutique next door, picked out four different blouses that enhanced the blue of Charlotte's eyes and matched the suit. Janine wasn't listening to any argument from Charlotte when she stepped out of the change room with the last blouse on.

"Charlotte, it is beautiful, fits you perfectly and matches your eyes."

"It does look good on me. It's just that it is so expensive."

"You will get lots of use out of it. You haven't updated your wardrobe for ages. Please, for me. Buy this blouse."

Later that day, Charlotte tried on the suit with the blouse and had to admit that, in her bedroom mirror, she looked professional and capable. She decided that her hair would need some attention to finish off the outfit and set her alarm to give herself enough time to style it before the interview.

"Charlotte." Irene knocked at the door.

Charlotte wasn't used to her mother knocking.

"Mother, how are you?" Charlotte stepped aside to let her mother in her home.

"How's the job hunt going?"

"I have an interview tomorrow."

"Is that what you are wearing?"

"It is," Charlotte waited for the usual reaction.

"It looks good on you. You look professional. I'm sure you will do well in the interview."

Charlotte had never ever heard her mother offer words of encouragement and could only stare.

"Aunt Alice offered me a job."

"But you won't take it, will you?"

"I didn't accept the offer." Charlotte wasn't sure why she answered with more of a maybe than a no.

"Good. You need to stay here where you were born. This is your home."

Funny, when her mother said it, the basement suite and Beckerville did not feel one bit like home.

twenty-five

. . .

"NOW, what shall we do with you?" Alice bent and scratched the top of the head of the little stray. Lucy had settled into life at the rescue shelter reasonably well. She wasn't as nervous and was comfortable with all the walkers. Alice had noted it was Charlotte who Lucy warmed up to the most.

"You two had a special bond, didn't you? A couple of hurt souls looking for someone just to love them." Alice grimaced at the thought of not being loved. She couldn't understand how Irene could show such carelessness toward Charlotte's feelings. Their interaction during Irene's brief stay was not what Alice felt a mother–daughter relationship should be, though Alice had little to go by. Beatrice hadn't been a nurturing mother. Alice wondered what having the love of both parents would be like. She and Charlotte were sure of only the love of one parent. They had that in common. Jim doted on his daughter, he told her as much when they spoke. The first time had been the year after her last visit. The one in which Irene told her to stay away.

"Alice, it's good to hear from you."

His voice sounded pleased. "How are you?"

"I'm good Jim."

"Are you coming this way?"

"You know I can't do that."

"Why the hell not?"

"You know."

"Well, Irene is wrong, and so was her mother. Oops, I guess Beatrice was your mother too."

"I agree with you. They are both wrong, but I don't want to cause any trouble."

"Well, you won't cause any with me, but I understand. It's not easy with Irene."

They chatted more, catching up about Charlotte. The conversations continued every month or so until Charlotte turned eighteen.

———

"It is Charlotte's graduation next week. Are you coming?" Jim wondered if that special occasion might prompt Alice to visit.

Alice considered his request. There was nothing she would have liked to do better. It would please her greatly to watch Charlotte cross the stage to receive her diploma, but suddenly appearing in Beckerville, after all those years, didn't seem the right thing to do. She hadn't seen Charlotte since she was eight years old, and she would have to deal with Irene in person.

"I just can't Jim. Give Charlotte a hug from me. There's a gift in the mail, addressed to you so Irene can't intercept it. What is Charlotte doing for the summer?"

"Oh, she has a job in town at the grocery store. Much to Irene's dismay. She said she didn't want her daughter bagging groceries and having all those old biddies in town gossiping with her, but Charlotte insisted. I was pretty proud of the way she stood up to her mother and took the job."

Alice laughed. "I'm sure Irene wasn't happy, but good for Charlotte. Did she apply to university?"

"She did. Your alma mater, is that what you call it?"

"The University of Alberta? Yes. I graduated from there. Is she taking education? I remember her telling me once she wanted to be a teacher."

"Well, she applied to the business school. Said she wants to be an accountant like you."

"Oh, that wouldn't have gone over well."

"No, it didn't. Irene said we didn't have the money to send her to university. Charlotte showed her all the scholarships she had applied for and which ones she already won. Irene's response was to tell Charlotte there would be no money from us for school. She was on her own."

"She can't help herself, can she?"

"No, I don't think she can. She seems to need to control everything about everybody and make it miserable when they don't heed her ways. Anyway, I later told Charlotte I had put money aside that her mother didn't know about for school and not to worry about the finances."

"If you need any more, just let me know. I have some set aside I would be happy to give her as well."

"Oh, we'll be fine, Alice, but thanks. I best go. I can hear Irene yelling for me. You take care of yourself."

"Bye Jim. Thanks for this. I'll call you soon."

"Do that."

Alice was grateful for those conversations. Grateful he was brave enough to talk to her behind his wife's back and grateful he was a loving father to Charlotte.

———

She remembered how wounded and sad Charlotte looked when she got off the plane in Victoria. Without Jim to protect her she wondered how much that wounded look was due to

Irene. She wondered if Irene bullied and badgered Charlotte because of what Beatrice made them do.

Lucy gave a nudge with her nose to remind Alice where she was. Alice continued to stroke the little dog's head. "Well, little foundling. I think you are going to be a permanent resident of this place. If Larry can live here, so can you. When Charlotte comes back, she will have someone to love." Alice went in search of Teresa to set up a spot in the house for Lucy to call her home.

twenty-six

· · ·

THE ACCOUNTING POSITION was what she was looking for, or at least what Charlotte thought she was looking for. There were possibilities for advancement like she didn't have at the other office, and the work looked challenging. She decided a fuller wardrobe was needed after her first week. She took her time by trying on over eight suits. Charlotte remembered Janine prodding her to try on clothes she might not otherwise have selected, and she was glad she had. She settled on two, one a deep burgundy, with a skirt, and second navy suit, this one with pants. Charlotte stopped at Janine's house after buying the new suits to show off her purchases.

"Wow. You clean up good. I like it. It makes you look smart. You've chosen some really great pieces."

Charlotte felt uncomfortable with Janine's compliments but pleased that she had chosen well. "I look just fine."

"You look great. Charlotte, your chances for advancement are better when you look like the job you want. You know you are capable of more than you have done. Certainly, more than Old Fuzziewig ever credited you for."

"I know. I do like how it looks, but I am not sure I can pull this off."

"Pull what off? You already have the job, and you know you can do the work. If you want advancement, then you need to look as professional as you can. Now, how is the apartment hunt going?"

"I still haven't started that again. More time with the company is needed before I'll have a reference for a lease application."

"Good enough. I'd like to see you out of that dingy basement suite. You are sure you don't want to go back to Victoria and work for your aunt?"

"That's all over. Remember, I said she was just being kind. I'll go visit her again. Maybe next year."

———

Charlotte thought about that next year time frame while at her desk the next day. She looked out the window beside the cubicle that was her office space. Her view was of buildings and a couple of small parks on the next block. She longed to get out of the office and walk on the grass, smell the air, and feel the sun on her face. She was pretty sure that leaving the task on her desk incomplete to walk in the grass would be unacceptable. If she had taken the job at the center, she knew she could have done that at any time.

She returned her attention to her desk and focused on the data she was reviewing. In her memory, she could hear the barks of the dogs in the pens and the chatter of the women as they went about their day. She shook her head again and refocused.

"Next year it will have to be," she resolved.

———

The days passed like that and after a month she felt like every day was like *Groundhog Day*, the movie. It was disheartening and discouraging. She quickly lost her excitement for the work. Completing analysis, discussing strategies, and writing business plans wasn't as engaging as she thought it would be. *Were they ever?* she wondered. *What do I do now?*

She thought about calling her aunt and asking her for advice. But given that she had declined her job offer, it embarrassed Charlotte to admit she was wrong. A stop at Janine's house was a better plan. "I am so grateful for you, my friend." The women hugged at the door.

"And I, you."

"I think I made a mistake taking this job. I hopped at the first offer."

"Why do you think you did that?"

"I wasn't sure that I would get another offer." Charlotte left the sentence unfinished.

Janine nodded in understanding. "What are you going to do?"

"I don't know. I just know I am not happy there."

"What does happy look like?"

"I am ashamed to say that it looks like working at the center with my aunt, walking dogs that I am petrified of, and living near the ocean."

"And ..."

"I would be embarrassed to call my aunt and ask for the job."

"Are you sure it would be that hard?"

"I was so adamant that I would not take it, I can't possibly call her back."

"If you are sure."

"Janine, I am sure. I am also lost, confused, mad, and sad. What am I doing with my life? I have a decent job that offers some future, yet all I can think of is walking dogs."

"Then why don't you go down to the animal shelter and volunteer?"

Charlotte stared at Janine. "You are right. That's all I need. I'll go there now."

————

Charlotte started walking dogs after an orientation session the following week. Then she shadowed one of the other volunteers. While the shelter wasn't like her aunt's rescue center, it had all she needed - dogs. The routine was very similar to what she knew.

Her first day, she cleaned out the pen and changed the blanket before taking a dog named Texas for a walk. Texas was an English bulldog, all forefront and a little behind. He was pleasant enough, tugged a little, but not so much that Charlotte couldn't handle him. They had a stroll around a designated path for walking shelter dogs. She had to stoop to pick up dog poo, and when she did, she paused and looked around. *That's better, now I feel like I am doing something I want to do.* Putting Texas away, she watched the dogs in other pens as their tongues lolled and their eyes watched her every move. She felt like she belonged somewhere for a reason.

The dog shelter seemed to be what Charlotte needed and work no longer made her feel unsettled. However, at supper with her mother the next day her unsettled feelings resurfaced.

The invitation surprised Charlotte, her mother rarely made her a meal since she had returned from Victoria. In fact, she couldn't remember when she last talked to her mother. She accepted the invitation out of curiosity and the potential to smooth the waters between them. Aunt Alice had suggested she should make some effort to better understand her mother.

"How's your new job?" Irene made chicken cordon bleu, a

dish that was one of Charlotte's favorites growing up. Another surprise.

"It's good. They've given me some new files. I guess after a month they have decided I am a good hire and do the work."

"Charlotte, you are just like your father. You don't know your own worth. You always needed so much propping up and I just don't do that. I am not good at complimenting people. Others have assured me that you are very good at what you do."

"Pardon me?"

"Your aunt told me how impressed she was with the work you did at the center. My friend Pearl's daughter Angie, works at your new firm, and she says they are all raving about you."

"They are?"

Charlotte wasn't sure what was going on. She felt like she had entered another universe. Her mother was being pleasant to her. What was going on?

"Mother, are you all right?"

"Yes, why do you ask?"

"You just paid me a compliment. I can't remember the last time you did that."

"Your aunt reminded me how short I can be sometimes and how that can come across to people. I wanted to make sure that you knew I admire you and am proud of you."

Charlotte nearly choked on her mouthful. Now she was sure she was in an alternate universe. She changed the subject. "What was it like, growing up?"

Irene turned her head to look out the window. She had a far-away gaze Charlotte didn't remember seeing before. "It was okay. I learned a lot of things from my mother. She was an excellent cook and kept a clean house and abundant garden."

"Did Aunt Alice learn those things as well?"

"She had other interests. She thought running a house was boring and spent more time with our father. After she went off to university, and we didn't see her much."

"University would have kept her busy."

"She made it clear she wasn't interested in coming back to Beckerville."

"How did my grandparents take that?"

"My father accepted it. He knew that all along. Your grandmother and Alice didn't get along about anything. She insisted Alice should return to Beckerville and work there after graduation. Alice did for a while but got out of Beckerville as soon as she found work elsewhere."

"Were you close?"

"We used to lie in bed at night and talk about our dreams. But when Alice started challenging Momma's expectations, things got rough. I wished Alice would just obey Momma, but she wouldn't. She said it was her life, not Momma's. I just tried to keep the peace between them, but that meant I had to side with Momma because she was the bigger force. We didn't need her to be mad at both of us. It was hard on our relationship. I felt like I lost my best friend, but it was easier with Momma when Alice left for university."

"Did you want to go to university, to have a career?"

"I hadn't thought about it much. I applied to go to technical school, to learn to cook. I also wanted to travel, but I only ever got to go to Victoria. Once."

"When Alice lived there?"

"Yes, a few years after she moved there. Momma and I went."

"For a visit?"

"More or less. You should get your aunt to tell you about it sometime."

"Why can't you?"

"Because it is her story to tell. Not mine."

Charlotte wasn't sure that was true. Since Irene admitted

she visited with Grandma, then Irene was there too. *Why was the story Alice's to tell? What was her mother hiding?* Charlotte couldn't imagine why her mother couldn't tell the story or at least have a conversation about it. But she knew the locked door look on her mother's face, and she knew it was time to finish supper and go back downstairs.

twenty-seven

. . .

SOMETHING ABOUT WALKING dogs changed Charlotte's attitude within the first week, and she found life better. Maybe it was the walks in the outdoors, or maybe it was the conversations she could have with the dogs that no one else heard. At work, her role continued to be challenging. And she was feeling brave enough to start the search for her new apartment.

Charlotte called Janine on the phone. "Come with me Janine. I need your eye to help me with this."

"I'm not sure I have time. The kids have a soccer tournament all weekend. Couldn't you book them during the week?"

"I want to see them in the sunlight."

In the background at Janine's house, Charlotte could hear her husband. "Janine, you can miss a game if that's what you need to help Charlotte. We can manage, can't we kids?"

Then she heard a collective "Yeah, chips and ice cream!"

"You didn't hear that," her husband yelled.

Janine laughed. "Well, looks like I can come. Why don't you pick me up and we'll grab a latte before we start? What time is the first appointment?"

They finished the logistics planning, and Charlotte hung up the phone. She could always rely on Janine.

The next morning was sunny which made Charlotte happy. Daylight would show an apartment at its best especially if there were lots of windows. A view would be nice too. While she loved her basement suite, she had not realized how much difference a view made to a home until she was at her aunt's place. That thought made her pause.

She hadn't heard from her aunt for a while. Charlotte was embarrassed they hadn't connected other than the text to say she arrived home safe. Why hadn't she called her aunt? Was it because she declined the job offer? That seemed a silly excuse when she and her aunt got on so well, so she made a note to call her aunt when she got home. She locked the door to her suite and turned. It surprised her to find her mother on the shared landing.

"Mother, I haven't seen you for a while? What have you been doing?"

"Oh, this and that. Nothing important. Where are you off to?" Irene talked like Charlotte's every move was her business, as if she was still underage. Usually, she caved and told her mother everything, but today she felt like some privacy.

"I am meeting Janine for coffee."

"Huh." Irene snorted. "When I was your age, we didn't have time or money for coffee. I had responsibilities. You have it so easy."

Charlotte wasn't sure how to respond to this remark. It said more about Irene than Charlotte, so she said nothing and continue toward her car. It surprised her to hear nothing more from Irene.

There were four apartments to look at. All within reasonable walking distance of work and a short drive to the animal shelter. She wanted to reduce the use of her car; in case it broke down. She couldn't replace it right now, but it was on her list.

Two of the apartments were in buildings with elevators and, although suitable, Charlotte ruled them out when they visited the third choice. It was a unit on the third floor of a four-story building with no elevators.

"But then you have to take stairs all the time." Janine observed.

"That's good for me."

"But what about moving?"

"I'll hire some movers. I don't want me or you to have to lift and carry anything. Besides, I don't have much." Charlotte visualized her basement suite and confirmed she had very little furniture.

"I guess. But if I were you, I would weigh it carefully. Stairs get old fast. I should know, I have my washer and dryer in the basement. All day long I go up and down those stairs. It's a good exercise class!"

"No mother needs exercise classes, Janine. It's us office workers that need to move more. We sit too long."

"The dog walking must make a difference."

"Remarkably it has. I feel better. The job isn't so bad anymore, and I'm not nearly as scared of dogs as I was. The time at Aunt Alice's helped me find better ways to handle them."

The third unit was everything Charlotte wanted. Large corner windows let in south and west light. There was one underground parking stall and a park a block away. The only drawback was the mint-green paint and carpet.

"Almost perfect." Charlotte winced at the color.

"It's a bit much, that's for sure. I wonder if you could paint the unit?" Janine winced too.

The rep from the management company replied to Janine's question. "Absolutely not. These are where is/as is rentals. No changes."

Charlotte looked at Janine, and they hurried through the rest of the unit.

"Well, that's not great. I don't think I can do mint green for an hour, much less for a year's lease." Charlotte said as they drove away.

Janine shook her head, laughing. "The look on your face was priceless."

"Well, the rep reminded me of my mother. A definite no. It would be like moving into the sunshine, but with a different cloud over me all the time. Let's go see the last one. Hopefully, it will be better."

But it wasn't. The unit was a corner unit on the second floor. It had lots of windows, but the view of a back alley and the windows of the building next door was disappointing.

"Well, that's that. I will have to live beneath my mother for the rest of my life." Charlotte exhaled in defeat.

"Oh, don't be silly. Let's do this again in a couple of weeks. I think it would be unusual to find what you want the first time."

"But it's not my first time. I've been looking for weeks. I'm just ready to get on with it."

"Regrets about not choosing Victoria?"

"Yes, and no. I miss being there, but I belong here. I would still have to look for an apartment there because I couldn't live with my aunt."

"I guess."

Charlotte dropped Janine off at the soccer field where the kids' tournament was being held. She drove home and sat in her car in the parking space, pondering what she had learned that day and the conversation with Janine. Maybe she was being hard on herself. Maybe she could cope with the rescue center work. She mulled that thought over as she walked up the sidewalk. There she found her mother sitting on the steps.

"Are you waiting for me?"

"I am."

"Why?"

"Your aunt has died."

twenty-eight

. . .

"WHAT HAPPENED TO HER?"

"I have no bloody idea. Someone named Sandy called me and just said she had passed away and the funeral is on Thursday." Charlotte thought her mother sounded almost defensive, like she had something to do with Aunt Alice dying.

"The day after tomorrow?"

Irene merely nodded.

"I have to call my boss." Charlotte hurried to her suite and locked the door. She didn't want her mother to witness what she did next.

Very calmly she called her boss to tell him she would be away for a few days. When she explained it was for a family emergency, his reluctance to accept her absence showed a little more compassion.

"It's like I take time off all the time," muttered Charlotte to herself. Once the call was done her calmness floated away, replaced by a churning in her stomach that she was sure would lead to her become sick. She held on to the counter while she let the nausea pass. Tears fell that she didn't stop. *I just found you, why did you have to go?*

Her next call was to Janine.

"Hi potato, how are you?" Janine was her usual bubbly self. Did anything ever get her down?

"Shitty. Are you home? Can you talk?"

"Just got home, the kids are in the tub and their dad is supervising. What's up?"

"My aunt died."

"Oh my. I'll be right over. Do you want to go for a drive or to sit at your house?" Charlotte almost laughed; Janine got practical so fast.

"Drive. I don't want my mother to be around. I'll meet you on the street."

Charlotte was relieved she timed her arrival on the curb as Janine pulled up. She turned her head and wasn't surprised to find her mother watching her from the window.

"Where to?"

"Can we go to the park out by the lake? There won't be so many people there and we can sit on the swings. You can watch me fall apart there. I just lost the best friend I ever had."

"Ahem," said Janine.

Charlotte chuckled. "Okay, second best friend." And then she cried.

Janine handed Charlotte tissues as she drove to the park. They walked to the swing set furthest from the parking lot and just sat with the tissue box in Janine's hand.

"What happened?" Charlotte was grateful Janine waited until she was able to talk.

"I don't know. Sandy called my mom to say she had passed and that the funeral is on Thursday. Oh Janine. What am I going to do?"

"Be grateful you went to the island and spent two weeks with her."

"I should have taken the job she offered."

"Maybe."

"What do you mean, maybe?"

"Just that. Maybe. I doubt taking the job would have impacted your aunt's health either way. This was sudden. Something else was going on. Something she didn't tell you."

"Why are there so many secrets in my family? Why does nobody tell me anything? Why did I have to lose someone so wonderful? Why didn't this happen to my mother?" Charlotte's eyes widened and her hand covered her moth. "I didn't mean that."

"It's okay honey. Your secret is safe with me."

Charlotte began to cry again and mopped up the tears with tissue after tissue.

As her energy sapped, the tissue pile on her lap grew more slowly until she held one in her hand that was barely moist. When her breathing returned to normal, she said, "Shit."

Janine's eyes widened. "Charlotte, I have never heard you swear before."

"Time and a place." Charlotte sniffed a couple of times and pushed herself to swing a little. "Now what do I do?"

"Go to the funeral, say goodbye to your aunt. And come back to Beckerville and live the best life you can. That's what she would want for you." Janine timed her swing to be in sync with Charlotte's.

"She would. It'll be hard."

"Yup." They both pumped higher.

"But I can do it."

"Yup." They pumped even higher.

"Thanks friend."

"Best friend."

They laughed and let the swings run out of energy until they came to a stop. They walked arm in arm back to the car.

Charlotte's stomach still churned but she could at least breathe normally. She met her mother on the landing.

"Charlotte? Are you all right?"

"No Mother, I am not."

"Is there anything I can do?"

"Haven't you always said how much you have already done for me? What more could you possibly do? You can't make Aunt Alice come back." Charlotte shut and locked her door.

———

Sandy picked Charlotte and Irene up at the airport the morning of the funeral. She was driving the Jetta. It was the first sign that something was different. Until then, it was easy not to believe Aunt Alice had passed. Charlotte took in a deep breath. It helped.

"Charlotte, and this must be Irene." Sandy hugged Charlotte and shook hands with Irene and opened the trunk for their luggage. "We are all so sorry for your loss."

"It's your loss too Sandy."

"It is. But you just got to know her. She hoped for much more time with you."

"Was she ill? She said nothing to me about being sick," Charlotte said. Charlotte looked at Irene in case she knew something, but Irene shook her head.

"Sorry, I thought you knew. The doctor diagnosed congenital heart failure a while ago." Sandy turned and looked at Charlotte whose face registered the shock she felt.

"No, I didn't know a thing. She said nothing. What else do you know?"

"She told me the last time she saw the doctor, he suggested she get her affairs in order. I believe that's why she reached out to you. She wanted to have time with you before she died. I don't think she was expecting it to be so short."

Tears came to Charlotte's eyes as she was hit again with what she had lost. She should have stayed on the island.

"I'll take you to the center so I can give you this car. Here are the keys to the apartment. You can stay there. Here are the phone numbers for her lawyer and the doctor for when you are ready. Your aunt had prearranged the funeral, so there are no decisions to be made. And I'll see you at the funeral this afternoon. Here are the details." The funeral program had a picture of Aunt Alice on it with Lucy in her arms. She was smiling. It brought tears to Charlotte's eyes.

The women were quiet as the car turned down the long lane to the rescue center. Everything seemed too clinical and unreal. Charlotte's heart softened when she saw Larry and was out of the car and hugging him as soon as Sandy had parked.

"Oh Larry," she cried. Larry just looked at her with slobber hanging out of his mouth and a lopsided grin. She stroked his head. Bonnie and Teresa came out of the house and offered their condolences and hugged Charlotte. Charlotte introduced them to her mother, and then they all stood and looked at their shoes. No one had any words. Charlotte noticed Irene stood off to the side, as if she wasn't part of this somber group.

"I'll take Mother to the apartment. We will see you this afternoon."

Thankfully, there was only an hour between arriving at the apartment and leaving for the funeral. Charlotte brushed the dog hair off her suit and stood on the deck, remembering the conversations she and Aunt Alice had shared as the sun set in the evenings. She almost cried again but inhaled to steady her breathing.

She found Irene sitting on the bed in Aunt Alice's room. She held a picture in her hand. It was of the two of them at Irene's wedding.

"This was on her dresser. I don't have this picture anywhere. Why would she keep this picture out? It is so old." Irene rambled but didn't look to Charlotte for answers.

"Mother, it's time to go."

———

The funeral home had a large reception area which was almost full when they arrived. Sandy introduced them to the funeral director. "This is Lori. She will lead the service."

"If you come with me, I will take you to the family room and lead you in after everyone is seated." Lori said. Irene and Charlotte found themselves in a small room with five wing-back chairs, a few tables and tissue boxes on all of them. Lori left them alone. Charlotte had nothing to say and kept the program for the funeral in her hands. She stared out the windows and thought about the joy and happiness that her aunt showed every day. The wait seemed to take forever, but ten minutes later, Lori returned to escort them into a larger room with benches and a front podium. She seated them in the front row.

Adjacent to the podium was a wooden table laden with bouquets in bright colors and a picture of Aunt Alice laughing with a dog under her arm. The dog was Lucy. Charlotte saw a tired look in her aunt's eyes that she hadn't seen before. Aunt Alice's eyes were not quite creased in merriment. Then Charlotte remembered that same look on her aunt's face on the sailboat when she had asked Aunt Alice if she was okay. It was not quite a smile. Like a cover up for what was going on inside. She wondered how Aunt Alice had deteriorated so fast in just a few short weeks. Or had it been there, and she didn't acknowledge it? Also on the table was a beautiful oak box. It glistened, reflecting the lights from above and the shapes and colors of the two women in the front row.

The music started. Charlotte looked around as if its choice was an error. Then she smiled. It was the rock-and-roll playlist that Alice kept on her phone and played everywhere —in the car, in the office, in the apartment. At the center, they would sing and dance to those songs. They were joyful and helped make this celebration of life brighter.

Lori stood at the podium to address the mourners. After outlining the sequence of events for the service, she invited Tim to speak.

"It is my honor to tell you about Alice today. I have known her just a few short years but wished I had known her longer." He talked about her work in the accounting firm and how she found her way to the center. And then he talked about the dogs' lives made better by the work of Alice and the people at the center. As he talked, a slide show played on a screen above and behind him, showing the pictures of the dogs with many of those in attendance. He finished his words with, "It delighted us when she reconnected with family in Beckerville and her niece Charlotte came for a visit. While all of us here and all our dogs think of Alice as family, we are happy that she had blood family too."

The slide show continued with the music in the background as Lori closed the funeral and escorted Irene and Charlotte to the large gathering room. Everyone followed. There was a screen hung on that wall displaying the same slides and music played.

"Wow, sixty some years, and all you get in the end is a twenty-minute service," Irene scoffed.

"Mother."

"Well, after all we live through, it's a pretty quick goodbye. I'm going outside, I'll find you later." Irene turned away from Charlotte, who didn't watch where her mother went. She wanted to be with the ladies from the center.

"Charlotte, how are you doing?" Tim put his arm around her and gave her a bit of a squeeze.

"Oh, not sure. It was such a surprise to meet her and now I have to say goodbye too soon. I wish I had known her longer. I wish I had taken the job." Tears welled in her eyes. She dabbed at them with a tissue.

"I know how you feel. She offered me the job as the executive director before she took it. I declined. I couldn't be a full-time vet and run the center. And I am the same. Wish I had taken it. Just to be around her more. She gave so much."

"She did."

"Are you here long?"

"I'm not sure, but I doubt it. I have a job now."

"Good for you. But someone will have to take care of her personal affairs."

"Oh, I'm sure she has lined someone up for that. You know Aunt Alice. She was always so organized."

"Well, maybe we could take a sail in her boat."

"After my last trip, I'm not sure that I would be any help."

"Of course you would be."

Lori joined them. "Charlotte, excuse me. Your aunt asked me to give you this envelope. It has the information you will need for tomorrow's meeting with your aunt's lawyer."

"But I'm sure I am not the executor."

"Oh, Tim is the executor." Lori confirmed and turned to Tim.

"I am. There will be a lot to go over, but let's wait till then. I'm off. I'll see you tomorrow." Tim gave Charlotte a hug.

"Is there anything else we can do for you or your mother?" Lori asked.

"What happens now?"

"Well, you can take your aunt's ashes home with you in the box. Or you can leave her here until you are ready to take her to her ultimate resting place."

"Oh. Where is that?"

"I think it is best that you learn that from the lawyer."

Charlotte gave Lori a puzzled look.

"Oh, no worries. I just think that the entire story is better than in bits and pieces. But you can take her home with you. She might like a few more nights at her apartment."

"I'll come find you before I go then."

Lori smiled and moved away.

Irene had returned from outside. Charlotte noticed that her mother's eyes were red.

"What did Lori want?"

"To know if we were taking Aunt Alice home with us today."

"Doesn't she go into a plot or something?"

"Are you uncomfortable if we bring her home with us?"

"What? Of course, I am. Aren't you?"

"Ah no. I wouldn't mind her in the apartment for a few more nights. Until we find out where she goes."

"When will we find out?"

"Tomorrow with the lawyer."

Charlotte retrieved the sacred box from the table and carried it with her while she visited with the center ladies. She gave it to her mother to hold for the return trip to the apartment, glancing at it frequently to make sure her mother was taking care of the precious box.

They placed Alice on the mantle and Charlotte double checked she was secure on that spot, fretting the box would fall and the contents spill onto the carpet. They found some soup in the cupboard and mostly played with it for supper. There wasn't any conversation. Both women were in their own thoughts, and not sharing them.

Irene went to bed first. They had barely spoken since they left the funeral. But Charlotte wasn't up for any conversation, so she had said nothing. When Charlotte took herself to bed she walked by her mother's bedroom and paused to knock and ask if she was okay. Her hand stalled millimeters from the door when she heard sniffling coming from within the bedroom. Charlotte wasn't sure she had ever heard her mother cry. It unsettled her so much, she didn't finish the knock.

She sat on her aunt's bed looking around the room, wondering what would happen to all its contents. She lifted the framed picture of the two of them earlier that year. Tim had taken it on the sailboat when they stopped for lunch. Charlotte could remember the feeling of the sun on her face and her aunt's hand on her shoulder. She remembered feeling happy that day. She didn't undress but rolled herself into the blanket on the bed and fell asleep slowly, wishing she could relive the past weeks.

twenty-nine

. . .

CHARLOTTE and her mother were alone waiting for Alice's lawyer after his assistant escorted them into the room, offered coffee and left. The two women had been silent all morning. Charlotte couldn't sit in silence any longer. She wondered aloud who would go through Aunt Alice's things, through her life.

"It won't be me." Irene was firm.

"What?"

"Oh, did I say that out loud? Oops." Irene's grin made Charlotte wince.

"What won't be you, Mother?"

"Alice's things. It won't be me clearing up her clothing or anything."

"You don't want to take care of your sister's things? You are her only relative."

"Well, you are too. Besides, I don't owe her anything."

"But you are closer than me. It should be you."

"Well, I'm sure your aunt had it all figured out, just like she had everything else figured out. Let's see what the lawyer says."

Charlotte was more worried about the rescue center and

what would happen to it. Dogs and people depended on its existence. She wondered what her aunt had in mind for that.

Mr. Stoddard entered the room and introduced himself to the two women. The assistant seated herself at the table and began typing on a laptop. She pushed a button that caused a screen to lower from the ceiling. Tim walked into the room and took a seat beside the lawyer.

"You all know each other?" Mr. Stoddard looked around the table. Everyone nodded even though Charlotte was pretty sure her mother didn't know who Tim was. "Now, let's get to this. Shall we?" His voice was very formal.

Charlotte liked Mr. Stoddard immediately. He reminded her of the rich man in the Monopoly game who dressed much the same. Mr. Stoddard's hair was white, and he had a goatee. His blue eyes had a glint, and he was short and wide. He wore a three-piece suit, something you didn't really see much anymore. There was a chain that ran from the buttonhole of his vest into a pocket, where she expected she would find a pocket watch. His smile was warm, and his tone was kind. He would have gotten along well with her aunt, she thought.

"Alice, your sister and aunt, was very specific about her will and what she wanted done with her effects. She has named Tim as executor, and we will cover details after I outline the key points. She wanted to tell you the details herself, so we planned for that."

"What are you going to do? Have a seance?" Irene laughed at her own joke.

Mr. Stoddard smiled indulgently. "We videoed her telling you what she wanted done. And I have a paper copy here." He moved his hands as if to pass the pages over, paused, then rested his hands on the table. "Let's play the video, first, and you can hear for yourself. We can then go over the details further on paper. Go ahead." He nodded to his assistant.

A black rectangle appeared on the white screen that covered most of the wall at the end of the table. It turned to light blue. Suddenly there was Aunt Alice. She looked good. Smiled even though the topic was serious. Charlotte's heart longed to reach out and hug her.

"Hello. Isn't technology great? I get to say one last goodbye and tell you my will myself. Then you can't have any doubts as to the seriousness of my message." Aunt Alice paused, looked down at her hands and then continued. "Irene, my savings account goes to you. Mr. Stoddard has the balance. Thank you for all that you did when Momma asked us to do the impossible. I know it changed the course of your life and you gave up a lot. If I could have stopped Momma I would have, but nothing could when she was intent on a plan. I know that money is no compensation for anything, but I hope it makes you comfortable for the rest of your life."

Mr. Stoddard nodded to his assistant to pause the video, and he handed a piece of paper to Irene. "This is the current balance. There will be deductions for final taxes, so this is not the final amount, and it will take some time before you get a check."

Irene's eyes widened as she looked at the papers before her. "Well, I never expected this. I don't know what to say." She looked at Charlotte. There were tears in her eyes. "Alice was very kind to me. I'm not sure I deserve this."

Charlotte wasn't interested in her mother's reaction. She wanted to hear more from her aunt.

"For you, Charlotte, I have something different. You are my sole heir, outside of the savings account for your mother. That means the rest of it: my house; my sailboat; the land and building of the rescue center; and the rest of the money and investments are for you. There is a list of personal items that I want to go to the women at the center, please take care of that for me. I would like to think that you would seriously consider taking on the rescue center as executive director, a full-time job. You have seen it now and know some of how it operates, and you know the people. I think you are the right person for the job, not just because you are my niece. I knew the moment you arrived in Victoria. I think you'll find there is enough in my investments to keep the center afloat and provide you with some financial security. Thank you for coming to visit when you did. It allowed me to put the last touches on this video before I died. Know that I love you and have always done the very best I could for you."

Alice sat back with a satisfied smile on her face. Charlotte thought she looked relieved as if she had completed everything on a long to-do list and was ready to rest. It confirmed in Charlotte's mind that Aunt Alice knew she wasn't well when Charlotte visited and was laying the basis for this video during that visit. She tried to remember all the things that she and her aunt had discussed during her visit. *Was there something she should have paid more attention to?* She was mulling this over when Mr. Stoddard cleared his throat.

"Charlotte, are you okay?"

"Oh, yes, I am. This is a bit of surprise. We only met again a couple of months ago."

"Well, in my mind, your aunt knew what she was doing. She was adamant you were the person she wanted to take over her work and her home. However, you don't have to. There are provisions if you don't want the responsibility. The final decision is yours."

Charlotte looked at her mother for help but realized that she had never asked for help from her mother. Why would she be doing it now?

"If you wish, we can review the paper will now."

Mr. Stoddard then went through the document page by page, outlining the details of Alice's holdings and the rescue center.

"It says here that she is only a partial owner in the land and buildings," Charlotte observed.

"That is correct."

"But it doesn't say who owns the other portion."

"That's me," said Tim.

Charlotte sat back. Suddenly she was owner of her aunt's apartment, and partner in a rescue center. All her problems in Beckerville seemed insignificant. The rest of her life lay in her hands. What was her aunt thinking? She couldn't stand in Aunt Alice's shoes. They were far too big.

thirty

. . .

"I'M sorry I wasn't at the funeral, Charlotte. Too much to juggle to get there. I'll pick you up at the airport and we can talk then. I'll get my mom to take the kids." Janine and Charlotte were chatting online the next day.

"No worries. I understand. Are you free now? I need to talk."

Janine yelled for the kids to put on a movie, and, like a switch, their noise went silent. The music of their favorite movie started to play.

"Okay. I'm yours. That will keep them entertained for a bit. Go."

Charlotte laughed.

"Well, it's a good sign that you are still laughing. It was so soon after your visit, I worried your aunt's passing would be hard."

"Oh, it's hard. Don't mistake that laugh for ease. I was just thinking about how fast you found something to amuse your kids. You are magical with them."

"Yeah, me and animated movies. Though there are cute characters, and the art is pretty, there are dark parts that need explaining. I don't want my kids having nightmares about evil crabs and lobsters."

"Kids movies have evil characters?"

"You need to brush up on your fairy tales."

"Well, I'll take care of that once I get everything here settled." Charlotte smiled. Calling Janine was the right thing to do, she already felt better.

"What's there to settle? Didn't your aunt have a will?"

"She did. And she left me everything."

"What's everything?"

"I now own half the rescue center, the apartment in Victoria, and have enough money to live a decent life."

"Wow."

"Yeah. A month ago, I was getting to know her again, and now I am the heir to her estate." Saying it made the responsibility and the impact sink in a little more. Charlotte wasn't sure if she felt happy, or sad, or both.

"What did your mother say?"

"Well, she cried."

"Over her sister's passing?"

"Aunt Alice left her a bunch of money and that seemed to satisfy her. You know mother and money."

"Well, that should solve her need for your rent."

"It changes things. That's for sure."

"Doesn't it mean you can now live your life on your terms?"

"It does, but I feel like I don't deserve this. I only got to know her again a few months ago and now I have more than I could ever want." Charlotte felt embarrassed by her sudden fortune.

"What are you going to do?"

"My first instinct is to move here, to the island. I love my aunt's apartment. It looks out over the ocean. Island life is so lush and fresh compared to life inland. I can have a new start here. Be a different me."

The thing about talking to Janine is that it makes you say what you are thinking, thought Charlotte. Charlotte surprised herself with how she badly wanted a new start.

"What is wrong with the old you?"

"Well, my landlord is oppressive."

"There is that. But that's not about you. And now you don't need a landlord."

"I don't. I feel I can start an actual life here. Be who I am supposed to be."

"Who is that?"

"The 'me' I discovered here on the island. Happier me."

"How did you find happier you?"

"I spent time with someone, who really loved me. I learned not to fear dogs. My heart has been fuller than ever before."

"So, what's in the way? Are you worried about your mother?"

"A little. She told me I owed her when I put her on the plane yesterday. I'm not sure for what."

"But you can't let that hold you back. Besides, it's always been about money for her. If your aunt gave her lots, why should there be any talk about needing more?"

"I'm not sure. She has always been looked after. I was next in line to do the job after Dad passed. Now that she can look after herself, she is in unfamiliar territory. Or maybe there is something I still owe her. I'll get that figured out later. For now, I need to focus on me."

"Anything in the way?"

"Well, the rescue center is also owned by the local veterinarian."

"Oh. What's she like?"

"It's a 'he'."

"Oh, tell me more. Someone your aunt's age?"

"No, more our age. He's kind with the animals, cares

about them. He and my aunt were close. It's Tim, the guy we went sailing with."

"So, the problem is ..."

"Janine, I'm worried that I am not enough for this challenge. I am used to taking pieces of paper and making sense of them for other people's businesses. I've not worked in an actual business before. I've only seen them on paper. I don't know if I have anything to contribute."

"Whoa there, girl. You should not walk away from this challenge. You are so much more than you ever gave yourself credit for. You won't be in this alone. There is staff at the center. They run the place too. I am very sure your aunt is in partnership with Tim because he is a fit partner. What are you worried about, really?"

"Um." Charlotte sniffed.

"Charlotte, it's okay. It is a lot. But you are up to it."

"I just don't think I can live up to my aunt's expectations of me. She entrusted me with all this and barely knew me. What happens if I mess it up and the rescue center must be sold? What happens if we can't find a place for all those dogs? I would be responsible for that."

"Charlotte Martin. You couldn't disappoint a saint."

Charlotte laughed.

"I'm serious, Charlotte. For as long as I have known you, I have been proud to be your friend."

"But this is different. This is about a business, and dogs. And my aunt. Why would she do this to me? Why would she give me all this responsibility?"

"I can't answer that for you, my friend. Perhaps Tim has some answers. Have you talked to him?"

"Not since we read the will. We meet again with the lawyer in a few days to go over things."

"Well, why don't you talk over coffee afterwards and see what insights he has into your aunt? There might be some clues there. In the meantime, what is your heart telling you?"

"Honestly? I didn't realize how happy I was here until I went back to Beckerville. I missed it so much, but it scared me to ask my aunt for the job she offered. To admit that I had made a mistake."

"There. You've said it now. You are where you know you will be happy. Go drink tea. Gaze at your view and get excited about a new life by the ocean. And trust your aunt's judgement. Oh, oh, Carol the crab is on the screen! Got to run. Love you lots."

Charlotte said a quick goodbye and clicked off the computer. She stood on the deck and breathed in the smell of sea salt. Listening to the chirp of the birds she smiled. This was a new beginning. What could go wrong if her aunt thought she was up to it?

thirty-one

. . .

CHARLOTTE SAT on the deck with a cup of tea, like Janine had suggested. She sipped and breathed in the salty tang of the ocean, thinking about a long-ago conversation with her aunt. It was on the last walk Charlotte and Aunt Alice took together in Beckerville. Charlotte had dared to ask Aunt Alice the biggest question she had ever asked anyone.

"Why is being a dutiful homemaker and cook so important to my mother and not to you?" Charlotte didn't want to show her aunt there was angst between herself and her mother.

"Oh, Irene was always interested in being an exceptional mother and housekeeper. Our momma thought it was the best characteristic a woman could have. And Irene believed her."

"Didn't you?"

"Oh, I believed it was one way a woman could be. But I knew very young it wasn't how I wanted to live. I wanted to explore, be unfettered, define my life."

"Did you get into trouble with your mother?"

"All the time. She used to make fun of my 'edumacation', as she called it. She thought I was too smart to be interesting to a man. She didn't think I would have a happy life with just a career."

"But you graduated university, anyway."

"I did. It was difficult. School work, a job to cover expenses that scholarships didn't cover. Four of us shared a big house to make it easier. But the library was my refuge. I worked hard there to get good grades. It was important to me. But it wasn't easy."

"I think I am more like you than my mother. Does that make sense?"

"Oh, more than you will ever know. You must be true to who you are. You need to decide what is important to you and stick to your guns. People say they love you and then say and do things to make you wonder sometimes. I just decided I knew what I wanted and just followed my dreams."

"It's hard when you are just a kid."

"It is. Everything is hard when you are a kid because you are learning so much but soon you will leave here and find what you want yourself."

Charlotte thought about that conversation as she walked to the kitchen of her aunt's apartment. Now *her* home. If she chose it.

She hadn't followed her dreams so far. She had done what was necessary. *Was this now her chance to follow her dream?*

thirty-two

. . .

CHARLOTTE PULLED BACK her hair into the ponytail again for the tenth time that day. *Cleaning out closets messes up your hair,* she thought. But the work was necessary and interesting. To move into her aunt's apartment, she would have to open some closet space. The bottom shelf was easy. Shoes for the donation bags. Her aunt had beautiful shoes that fit size eight feet, not Charlotte's dainty size sixes. It was sad to see them go, but at least they were being gifted to other people. The clothes hanging in the closet were just as easy, too snug for Charlotte, so were folded and placed into boxes, again for a charity donation. Charlotte next tackled the top shelf, pulling boxes down one by one onto the floor.

The first box was red, about the size of a piece of paper and about four inches deep. There was a clasp on it that opened easily. The box was of rigid cardboard, alluding to valuable contents. Charlotte opened the lid and found a jumble of things: some envelopes, a tiny cloth bag that was not empty, and a handful of pictures. Thinking it was time for a break, she took the box and its contents into the kitchen and put the kettle on the stove.

With tea in hand, she sat at the table and took out the

pictures first. She glanced through them, trying to find familiar faces. The first picture was Aunt Alice and a man by the water. Charlotte thought she recognized the harbor front. A few of the buildings had changed since the picture. Written on the back were the words "Pete and me, May". The year noted was the year before Charlotte was born. She stared at the picture, trying to find meaning in the photo, but it appeared to be just her aunt and a man. Someone Aunt Alice liked. They were both smiling with arms flung around each other.

The second picture was Aunt Alice alone, at about the same age, sitting amongst the flowers in a garden. She was looking off to the side of the camera as if unaware of the picture being taken at all. And on the back was written "My rose". No date.

The third picture was her aunt in front of the sign for the rescue center—a wooden sign carved in relief painted black with cobalt blue words that read "The Dog House". She was in a suit and stood proudly beside the sign. On the back was the word "owner".

The rescue center still had the same sign today. Charlotte had remembered the story her aunt told of putting it up and being the owner of something bigger than herself. How it made her believe in who she was. And finally believe that what she did was meaningful for those in need.

The last picture was of the same man, Pete, standing by the docks. He stood proud and tall. He wore a bright red jacket and what looked to Charlotte like thick snow pants. There was a knitted toque on his head, and he held a pair of thick gloves in his hands. The sky behind was grey. Charlotte shivered, thinking it must have been a chilly day. Written on the back was "Race Day". Charlotte wondered what had happened to Pete. Aunt Alice never mentioned his name in any of their conversations.

The cloth bag was next. The first thing she pulled out was

a pink card. On it were various details of a baby's birth—name, date, weight, length. Only some details were legible. On the bottom was the name of a hospital in the city.

This is the card put in the bassinet for a newborn, thought Charlotte. She remembered similar one when she had visited Janine after her daughter was born. The name *Alice Knight* was on the line for Mother.

Charlotte creased her forehead. She didn't realize her aunt had had a child. She peered at the date closer to see if she could find out when. But it was too faded. Charlotte flipped over the card, hoping for more of an explanation there. But the back was empty.

She next pulled out a picture of a baby wrapped in a blanket lying in a crib. The picture was black and white, and the surroundings were not familiar. There was nothing written on the back. She reached into the bag for the next item. It was a tiny rattle. She jiggled it to see if it still worked. It did. The last item in the bag was a locket the size of a quarter, but an oval shape. It was gold on the outside and when Charlotte pried it open, it revealed a place for two pictures, one on each side. A tiny baby face on one side and a curl of hair on the other. Charlotte wondered who the baby was. There were no clues on the back of the locket.

Engraved on the front of the locket in cursive were the letters C. K. Charlotte wished she knew what all these artifacts were about. *Were they connected to Pete? Was this Aunt Alice's child? Did her mother know about this?*

Charlotte felt sad when she acknowledged as close as she and her aunt were, they had discussed none of this. Why hadn't her aunt confided in her during their time together? Another secret kept from Charlotte.

Charlotte carefully placed the items back into the bag and into the box and set it aside. She gazed out the window as she sipped her tea. She and her mom would have a long talk when they were together in the next couple of days. Charlotte resisted picking up the phone to call. This wasn't a conversation for over the phone. It must be face to face.

She remembered the second box on the bed, and she brought it to the table. In it were two letters addressed to Alice from Irene. The dates were not long after Charlotte was born. Irene wrote in both how well Charlotte was doing, smiling, and cooing, and how much she loved being a mother. Charlotte smiled. It wasn't a feeling Charlotte remembered her mother sharing with her.

She was a little stiff from the work she had done that morning, so she put the letters and other items into the cloth bag into her backpack for her visit to Beckerville. She hoped her mother would reveal what Aunt Alice kept secret.

She put on her runners and a sweater and headed for the beach.

thirty-three

. . .

TWENTY-EIGHT YEARS EARLIER.

"Alice, how are you? Is everything okay?" It was early in the morning and Alice usually called in the evening. Irene had just finished the outside chores and was preparing breakfast for Jim and herself. Spring was underway, yet the leaves were still buds, but promising greenery within days.

"No, everything isn't okay."

"Oh dear, what happened?"

"There was a sailboat race yesterday, and it was freezing. The winds were fierce, and the waves were huge. The sailboats had trouble getting back to the marina when they called off the race. Pete's boat didn't make it. They tried to save the crew and the boat but saved only two people. Pete ... he drowned. He didn't have a chance. Two other boats lost men too."

"Oh, Alice. I am so sorry. Are you okay? Do you want me to come there?"

"No, no, I'm okay, it's still new, I'm still adjusting but there won't be a wedding now. Can you tell Momma?"

"Um, sure, I can do that. Are you sure there isn't anything else I can do?"

"No. That's plenty, I don't want to face Momma over this. She won't be kind."

"Sure she will."

"No, she won't. She hasn't an empathetic bone in her body."

"But this is different. It is serious."

"She won't be kind and I can't deal with it."

"I'll take care of it. But I think you are wrong."

"Say what you like. I got to go. I'll call you in a few days."

"Please do that. Love you, Alice."

"Love you too, Irene."

———

It surprised Irene that Alice was right. She called Momma right after hanging up from Alice's call.

"Well, what happened?" Beatrice demanded. But before Irene could say anything she asked, "Did he leave her? I knew it wouldn't last. I knew it wasn't serious."

"Momma, how can you say that?"

"Well, your sister didn't want marriage and children, anyway. She is a career woman. They don't have time for, what did Alice call it, the simple family life."

"You can have a job, a marriage, and children. A woman can have it all." Irene insisted.

"Well, apparently they can't because Alice doesn't have it anymore. It's just as well, we couldn't afford the wedding any way."

"Momma, we could too. And you know Alice and Pete were paying for most of it."

"Well, it saves us a lot of money that we can sure use on the farm. And we don't have to make that long trip to the island. I, for one, am glad."

"But Alice lost Pete. How can you be so cold about her losing the man she loved?"

Beatrice sniffed. "How do you know he loved her?"

"I know."

"How do you know?"

"Momma. Pete and Alice were going to be married. They loved each other and wanted to spend their lives together. Isn't that enough?"

"People get married for reasons other than love. More practical reasons."

"Like what?"

"To be help mates with each other. To be a team. Because they have common goals."

"Was that why you and Dad got married?"

"I married your father because he asked me to."

"Didn't you love him?"

"I didn't have time for love. I looked after my sick mother, and then my brothers and my father after she died. When my brother got married and brought his wife to the house, I had to leave. I had to find a life of my own. I couldn't go back to university, so I married your father."

Irene's face registered the shock she felt at hearing this story for the first time. She knew her momma looked after her mother when she was sick, but she didn't realize what her momma gave up providing that care.

"I didn't know you went to university. What did you take?"

"I was going to be a teacher, a science teacher. But then Mother got sick, and that dream died."

"But you could have gone back."

"It was too late; I was too old. And besides, it was time to get on with life."

Irene yearned to hear more. Her mother had never shared tales of her earlier life before.

"Did you and Dad know each other?"

"He was a good friend. Their farm was down the road. He liked to fish and to farm. He was always there when I needed him. It seemed like the right thing to do to get married."

"You loved him though."

"We had a life to live, a farm to run, and eventually you and your sister. He was a good man."

"But you loved him."

"I don't know what love is. We got along and we knew the roles on the farm. Is that the way you feel about Jim? Do you love him?"

"Yes."

"Well, your father offered me a life beyond my parents' house."

"But he loves you."

"No, he doesn't."

"Yes, he does, I can tell. Why are you so hard on him?"

"Am I?"

"You are Momma, you are hard on all of us."

"Well, that's just my way. You just have to deal with it."

Irene felt the door that peeked into her mother slam shut. She was pretty sure it wouldn't open again. It left her wondering whether she knew how to love.

———

Alice and Irene traded phone calls once a week for the next month until Irene was sure Alice was okay. Irene was happy Alice was busy with work, she was sure that it helped ease the pain. But she knew busy wasn't likely enough to ease all of it. She didn't tell Alice about Momma's reaction. Alice had predicted it.

———

Time went on. Irene was busy dealing with her own problems. No matter how much they tried, she and Jim couldn't conceive. The doctors couldn't find anything particular in their way. They discussed fertilization but didn't have the extra funds. They put off discussions on adoption, although inevitably, they would have to, at some point. She didn't want to share the pain of not being pregnant with Alice until she was sure Alice was over her own grief. But when would that be?

One day, three months later, she thought it might be time. She called Alice.

"Hi Alice, how are you doing?"

"Ok. Better. And then sometimes not. How are things with you and Jim? Pregnant yet?"

"No. Seems things don't work well in that department."

"It can't be that bad."

"Alice, it's been two years and nothing. I don't think we are going to have children."

There was silence.

"Well, I am." Alice said quietly.

"What?"

"I am going to have a baby. Well, Pete and I are going to have a baby."

"Oh Alice, how lovely. Are you okay about it?"

"I am. I can have a part of him with me now." Irene thought she heard contentment in Alice's voice.

"But how are you going to raise the baby? You work full-time."

"I'll manage. There is good care in the city. It will be okay."

"Are you sure? Sounds like a lot."

"I'll be fine. But don't tell Momma. I will find my own time to tell her."

"It's your story. Count on me to keep the secret. Will you tell me when you are close? I will come and stay with you?"

"You'd do that?"

"I will. Promise." Irene was sincere.

"I'll hold you to that."

"You better. It will be fun. I'm looking forward to meeting my niece or nephew."

"You don't wish it was you?"

"Me what?"

"You being pregnant."

"It is what it is. Besides, you are the next best thing. As long as you think you will be all right."

"I will be."

"You'll tell me if you aren't. Right?"

"Right. Listen, got to run, work and stuff."

"Chat soon."

Irene hung up the phone, pondering what she had just learned. Not telling Momma was fine with her. She didn't want to be around when Beatrice found out that Alice was having a baby with no Pete in the picture.

thirty-four

. . .

CHARLOTTE PULLED into the parking lot of the center the next day and turned the car off. She sat for a while, trying to arrive at her new location in mind and body. It was hard.

"I don't know why you did this to me, Aunt Alice. Why do you think I can do this when I'm not sure I can? I don't want to fail your trust."

Charlotte smiled, remembering that not so long ago she wanted a promotion that would give her more responsibility. And here she was, by a circuitous route, with increased responsibility. She had an urge to scurry into the building and shut herself in the office. But that would not go over well. Charlotte firmly shut the door of the car and walked as boldly as she could to the back door. She tripped on a rock and muttered to herself. "So much for confidence."

Charlotte quietly opened the door, wishing no one would hear her or greet her as she entered the center. She had to pass by the kitchen on the way to the office and as she approached the door, she heard murmurs.

Well, might as well get this over with. She stopped in the kitchen's doorframe.

"Charlotte," Teresa was first to rise from the table and greet her with a warm, long hug. "How are you, dear?"

"I'm okay."

"Well, good. That's a start then, isn't it? Come on, we just brewed a pot of tea, you look like you could use a cup."

Gratefully Charlotte sat down, sipped from the mug offered to her, and helped herself to a cookie from the plate in the center of the table.

"We brought some cookies from the funeral here." Teresa looked at Charlotte with an apology on her face.

"Good idea. I didn't even think."

"No one expected you to dearie." Sandy touched Charlotte on the arm. Charlotte smiled at Sandy, realizing how warm it felt to have caring people around.

"We honestly didn't expect you here so soon." There were nods around the table.

"It seemed it was time."

"Did you go back to Beckerville after the funeral?"

"I'm going there tomorrow. I think this is home now. Is that weird?"

"No. We knew the first time we saw you, you would end up here. But you left, then your aunt passed ..." Sandy let the sentence end unfinished.

"But you expected me back."

"Well, Alice told us her plan for the center for when she passed."

"You knew she wasn't well?"

"Yes, dearie. She felt it only fair that we knew she could leave us quickly, and she wanted us to feel safe in the work here. She swore us to secrecy. We weren't to tell you. You won't change things, will you?" Sandy's face looked concerned.

"No, I'll change nothing. You have been doing this for so long, I feel like I would be in the way."

"Not a chance, Charlotte. You know there is usually more

work than hands around here, and someone must be at the helm to make it all work. We know you will figure it out. And we are all here to help. Just ask." Teresa's voice was consoling.

A tear slid down Charlotte's cheek. She was not used to kindness from anyone, and these women were almost strangers.

"Thank you," was all she could manage. "I think I'll go to the office now."

No one interrupted her leaving the kitchen. Charlotte heard chairs scrape and dishes being put in the sink as she walked down to the office. She opened the door and stood at the threshold, taking in all that was now hers. It was sparse but filled with pictures, as was the hallway—she had never been sure whether the pictures of former rescues started here and then flooded the hallway or the other way around.

She moved to the window and looked out at the open cages where everyone was placing the dogs for their time outside. She heard a rustle behind her and turned to see Lucy wagging her tail.

"Hello, sweetie. I didn't expect to find you here." Charlotte bent and rubbed Lucy's head.

"Well, Alice decided I got to stay."

Charlotte stood up quickly, recognizing Tim's voice. He stood in the doorway.

"Your aunt decided Larry needed some company. And she thought you would like to have Lucy as a companion."

Tim stood quietly, watching Charlotte's face. She felt like he was looking for something.

"I would." Charlotte bent down to stroke Lucy's head. Lucy licked her hand. "Have a seat." Charlotte pointed to the table.

"How are you doing? I bet you are tired of people asking you that question."

"So tired. I am okay. One step at a time. Right?"

"That's all you get."

"Tell me, did you know she wanted me to take over her role at the shelter?"

"Yes. She talked to me about three months ago. I wasn't sure she was doing the right thing giving it over to a relative stranger until I met you. Then I figured she had made an excellent choice."

"Did she offer it to you?" Charlotte ignored the compliment.

"We already share ownership in the facility and the land. I was happy to continue as advisor. With a full-time vet clinic to look after, I can only be here for medical support and the sailing, of course. I helped a lot when she first started, but as time went on, she really relied on me as a sounding board. The staff know what they are doing. I am almost window dressing now."

"Well, I doubt that, but I will need to lean on you for help since I am in this, whether I want to or not."

"Do you want to?"

"I'm not sure." The wavering in her voice surprised her. She thought about that for a minute before she continued. "It seems like a lot. I found some strategy documents in the files. Do you have time to go over them sometime? Maybe that will help me decide."

"Why not right now? Let me grab a cup of tea and I can give you an hour now. We drew those documents up last year, some things may have changed. And if we need more time, we can figure that out later." He turned to leave.

Charlotte was pulling the binder off the shelf when she heard a yelp, a howl, and a scream. Tim beat her down the hallway and through the door.

It hadn't been like this when her aunt was here those weeks ago. In fact, the place was usually placid. *Was it already falling apart?*

thirty-five

. . .

THE CHAOS before her eyes was hard to sort out. There seemed to be loose dogs all over the place, most of her staff were running after them, and Tim was holding down one dog that seemed in trouble. Pens were open and Teresa was sitting on the ground, with a cloth wrapped around her hand. It was slightly red. Charlotte watched. "Teresa, are you alright?"

"I am now that Tim has Fred under control. Something happened between him and Barney and then he snapped at me. And Barney took off. Sandy and Bonnie ran off to find him."

"Do you know why all the pens are open?"

"Yeah, everyone was leashing the other dogs to go for walks, and this interrupted them. We all panicked and instead of shutting the gates to the pens, we left some open. Bonnie and Sandy are also chasing Jango and Chutney," Teresa admitted.

"Did someone call 911 for you?"

"I'll be fine, don't worry about me. It's only scraped badly, no bones broken."

"No, you need that looked at. Once we get the dogs sorted, we will get you to the clinic or call 911. You decide."

"Go find those other dogs and then we can get me to the emergency room. I'll keep this elevated and wait for things to settle down." Teresa sat on the chair by the back door.

Charlotte watched as Tim ran his hands over Fred's forelegs and back. "Tim, is Fred okay?"

"He is, no marks or cuts, not sure what Barney was about, but we can get into that once we find him."

"Okay, then I'm off to help Bonnie and Sandy finding our escapees. Can you put Fred back in his pen? I'll be right back."

Charlotte set off with a leash. She met Sandy and Bonnie with Jango and Chutney individually leashed and separated. "Are they okay?"

"We think so. They really looked like they were just happy to be running free. Opportunists, them." Sandy laughed.

Charlotte frowned.

"I know it's serious. But honestly, if you saw the look on their faces when we found them, it was like capturing truant school children. Glad for the experience, unhappy to be caught."

"I get it. Get Tim to have a look at them in case there is something we haven't noticed. Any sign of Barney?"

"No, we didn't even catch a glimpse. But the property isn't that big, he can't be far. Let us know if you need any help. Just give us a yell." Bonnie and Sandy headed back to the pens.

Charlotte called Barney's name as she wandered closer to the further edges of the property. It was a while before she heard anything, and only then it was a whimper. She called his name again to help her locate the whimper and finally she saw Barney's white butt sticking up by a fallen tree.

"Barney," she called, but he only whimpered back. It looked like he couldn't move.

Charlotte moved herself beside Barney, looking for clues for how he had lodged his head. She moved to the other side and then tried to get herself in front of him, but the large tree, that was partially responsible for the cave that Barney had his head stuck in, was impossible to get around.

"Well, my dear. You have yourself tightly tucked into something, haven't you?" She ran her hand over his back to see if she could get him to lie down instead of standing.

"You are a good boy, and we will get you out of this, no worries. How about you lie down?" Charlotte's voice was soft as she stroked him. She felt the muscles on his back ease and then watched as he lay himself down, but his head wasn't coming out of the hole easily. She moved her hands around the sides of his face, telling him what a good boy he was, how patient he was being. Overhead, a squirrel chattered as if mocking the dog. Charlotte wondered if the squirrel had played a role in Barney's head getting stuck.

She carefully nudged him this way and that until he could back himself out the rest of the way. She grabbed his collar and attached the leash to him. It was only then that she noticed he had three long porcupine quills piercing his nose. The squirrel continued to chatter.

"Oh Barney, no wonder you were so mean to Fred. Come here, let me look at those." Charlotte peered at the quills, knowing that she wouldn't dare pull them out, but she knew exactly who could. "Come on, let's go find Tim. He'll help you out."

Within an hour, Teresa's hand was properly bandaged. Barney's nose was quill free, thanks to Tim, and with some regular salve application would be fine in no time. Charlotte sat with the staff and went over what happened and planned out how they could have handled it all better, if there was a next time. But they all hoped there would not be.

In the end they all laughed, because three porcupine quills had turned a normally quiet center into a circus. They searched the fence line and found a hole just big enough for the porcupine. Charlotte found a piece of wood and fastened it to the fence with some zip ties to keep out further wanderers. They would deal with a permanent fix the next day.

"I'm glad it was only that. Thanks everyone, I'm calling it a day." She waved goodbye, relieved that she could leave early. It was hard enough visiting the center that day, but the excitement reminded her that not every day would be idyllic.

On her way home, she stopped at the vet clinic to talk to Tim about Barney.

"He'll be fine. Probably his pride hurts more than his nose. Give him a couple of days. How about those plans we were going to discuss? Did you want to go over them now?"

"No, I've got to get home and pack."

"You're leaving us?"

"Just for the weekend. I'm going back to Beckerville to see my mother about a few things."

"Back next week?"

"Tuesday. How about we get together on Wednesday, Tim, and see what you and my aunt were planning?"

"That works. Your aunt would be proud of how you handled things today. You took care of everyone, and you got a dog out of a hole in the ground. You've come a long way." Tim shared.

"I have, haven't I?" Charlotte almost skipped out of the vet clinic.

———

She was still humming when she arrived at her mother's house the next day. That radiant energy vanished when she sat down with a cup of tea and the letters that she had opened earlier. She wanted to hand them to her mother, but before they went over them, she wanted to find out about the last conversation she knew of between her mother and Aunt Alice.

"Mother, I don't understand what Aunt Alice meant about things not being my fault."

"When did she say that?" Irene asked.

"I heard it the morning we went to the center. What were you two talking about that morning and what wasn't my fault?"

thirty-six

. . .

"CHARLOTTE, this is so complicated and so old. What went on between Alice and me was a long time ago."

"She said it wasn't my fault. I don't understand what that means. Is that why you were always so hard on me? What did I do wrong?"

"I was difficult on you?" Irene spat out the words. "Charlotte, do you have any idea what it is like to live your life according to your mother's plan? Without choice? Without hope of having anything you want?"

"You had Dad, and he was a good husband. You never seemed to have to sacrifice. What choices did you miss out on?"

"Your grandmother made it so that I could never have a career. I could never hope to be more than just a farm wife."

"I thought you enjoyed being a farm wife."

"I did. I knew I wanted to stay on the farm and work in the yard and the garden. I loved that life. At least I thought I did." Irene got up from the table. She moved to the small cupboard above the refrigerator and pulled out a bottle of scotch. It had the same label as the one Charlotte had found in her aunt's apartment.

"Mother, that is the same brand that Aunt Alice drinks."

"I know, she gave this bottle to me, long before you were born. We used to sit on the deck in the summer night and sip a drink and talk about life. I quit drinking it when she didn't come around in the summer."

"Why did she stop coming?"

"I asked her to stop."

Again silence.

"I'm not sure where to start. There are so many layers to the story that got us here today. I guess it is time that you know the whole truth and then you can understand why things are the way they are. But remember, I wanted to tell you earlier. Alice wanted it this way." Irene's shoulders sagged as she sat at the table and held her hands together.

"I'd like the truth. Maybe then things would make sense. Like why Aunt Alice left me everything and why didn't anyone tell me I had a cousin?" Charlotte couldn't wait to find out about that.

"What makes you think you have a cousin?"

"This." Charlotte handed Irene the pink card she found in her aunt's belongings.

"Oh." Irene held the card for what seemed like a very long time. She took a sip of the scotch. She stared into the glass, at the card, and then at Charlotte.

"Let's start with me first. When we were young girls, the neighbor's dog had a litter. I asked Momma if we could have one. She was talked into it by Dad. Momma only saw it as work. But it was one of the kindest things she ever did for me. I was responsible to clean up after him and feed him. I named him Cooper. He was lovely. I would sneak him up to bed with me and we would snuggle. The world felt whole and fabulous. We would be together all the time I was not at school. I got into trouble lots at mealtimes until I taught him to not sit under my chair. He was everything to me."

"What happened to Cooper?"

"Unfortunately, he liked to dig in the dirt, and one day he dug up Momma's flowerbed, when I was at school. He wasn't there when I got home. Momma said we couldn't have a dog that dug up the yard and she got rid of him."

"Did she tell you where?"

"No, I didn't get to ask anything. He just disappeared. Something I loved so much was suddenly gone."

"That must have been sad for you."

"It was. I felt like I had lost my arm. I was sad for months."

"What did Grandma Beatrice say? Was she sorry?"

"Nope, Momma said it was my fault Cooper got into trouble. I hadn't trained him well."

"Did she ever say anything about him after that?"

"No."

"Did she ever have a pet of her own?"

"I don't think so. All we ever heard about her childhood was how much work she did. Never about happy things. She was the eldest and the only girl. There were eight kids, so she helped with everything. I think she had little pleasure in her life. I'm not even sure I ever saw her smile." Irene paused, wiping the corners of her mouth. "And no matter how hard I tried; I couldn't make her smile. I did everything she showed me, everything she asked. She barely talked to me. We worked a lot together in the kitchen and garden but never talked. It was a very silent world. If I asked her a question, she would give me a very sharp answer, and that was it. I don't think we ever had one conversation."

"Where was Aunt Alice?"

"Avoiding Momma. She spent her time in the fields and barns with Dad. The only time she dealt with Momma was at mealtime."

"But you were close." Charlotte said.

"We were. We would lay in bed at night and talk about life. What we wanted to do, where we wanted to go. Alice always knew she would leave and go to university. It wasn't that clear for me. I thought I would always be on the farm. I wasn't sure about life. I wasn't like Alice."

"Sounds lonely."

"I never thought about it like that. I guess it was. Then I met your dad. I was about fourteen when he moved into the area, and we became friends. We rode the school bus together. The teacher asked me to help him on his first days. He wasn't Cooper, but at least he was someone I could talk to a bit. He was shy. We spent most of our time together. We helped each other with our chores, and we played on the same ball team. He had such dreams for his farm. He made me see I could have dreams too. I started to think I could have a life with him when a new girl moved into town. He caught her eye, and she decided he was hers. And just like that, he was gone. No more baseball, no more chores, no more dreams."

"What did you do?"

"I just got on with life. Something else I loved was taken away from me. I figured I wasn't pretty enough to turn his head. It left such a hole. I don't remember ever hurting so much before."

"But you got married."

"Something happened between them. I think his brother became the better catch when he was accepted to dental school. I guess she thought that was a better future for her than being a farmer's wife."

"Then what happened?"

"I started seeing him around and we became friends again. But I didn't tell him how much I loved him. I didn't want to hurt that way again, ever again. I was always scared someone else would come along who he would love more."

"Did he say anything?"

"No. Not really. We just took up where we left off. One day he asked me to marry him."

"Just like that?"

"Yeah."

"What did you do?"

"I said yes fast before he changed his mind. It was impossible to live around Momma and I needed a way out."

"So, you married for love."

"What?"

"You said you loved him."

"What is love, Charlotte? I married your dad because we were friends, and we like the same things about life. He was safe. He was a way out of the house. Momma and Dad approved of him. I wasn't going anywhere, so it was the simple thing to do."

"Did you ever have a job?"

"I wanted to get a job when I was in high school, but Momma said no. She said that I would need to be picked up and that wouldn't be convenient, even when both Dad and Jim said they would come get me. She said that her daughter wasn't going to work in a silly little job in town waiting to get married. Once I was married, I would stay at home, anyway."

"Gramma had some pretty hard ideas."

"She did."

"Why didn't you just do it, anyway."

"I don't think you ever saw your grandmother when she got mad. There is one time I can remember when I was about twelve. I had a book that I was returning to the neighbors, they had kindly let me borrow it. I told Momma I was going down the road to drop it off and I would be back soon."

"What happened?"

"She got mad. She started yelling and throwing things and saying words I don't remember. I just remember the tornado that she became. It scared me."

"What did you do?"

"I ran out of the house. Luckily Dad was in the shed working on the tractor. He saw me running and asked me what was up. I told him about Momma."

"What did he do?"

"I remember this look in his eye, like he was watching a movie in his memory. He gave me a hug and said it was best to dry my eyes and take some breaths. To get on over to the neighbor's and return the book. 'Mind you smile,' he'd said."

"Cover it up."

"Yeah, we did a lot of that. Momma didn't have many of those spells, but we always acted like they never happened and just got on with our days."

"What was your mother like when you got back?"

"She acted like it hadn't happened. She wouldn't look at me at first, and then when she did, she was defiant. Like there couldn't possibly be anything the matter with her. Like I was the problem."

"Wow? What do you think it was that caused her to act that way? Was she imbalanced?"

"I was never completely sure. It might have been about loss of control. She didn't want me growing up and becoming independent. She wanted me to be at her beck and call all the time. To make a choice for myself was not in her game plan. She had no control over Alice and she would not have the same with me, I guess."

"Oh Mom, I am sorry."

Irene's head turned quickly to stare at Charlotte.

"You've never called me Mom."

"What? I have too."

"No, you always call me Mother."

Charlotte's face squeezed tight, as if remembering every time she spoke to her mother.

"I guess I do."

"I always cringed when you did. It was what I called my mother, and I didn't want us to have that same relationship. Mother sounds so stiff and formal. Mom always sounded softer and more loving, but you never used it."

"It wasn't conscious."

"You always called your father Dad."

"I did."

"Why?"

Charlotte took a deep breath and let it out. "He was more loving."

"He was. He doted on you. Even though you weren't his." Irene's eyes widened. She gasped. Her hand moved to her mouth as if to put back what she had just uttered. There was only silence in the room, as the two women sat facing each other across the table.

"What do you mean I wasn't his?" Charlotte's voice was tiny, in fear of what she had always known, that she didn't belong to this couple.

"You weren't mine either."

"What do you mean, Mother? Was I adopted?"

"Well, sort of."

"How can I be 'sort of' adopted?"

"It was clear early on after we married, we would not have children. Something wasn't working. We went to several doctors who couldn't pinpoint any problem. They suggested we consider fertility treatment or adoption. The former we couldn't afford, and the latter just didn't seem right."

"How did I get here?"

"From Alice."

Charlotte's eyes moved to the pink card still lying on the table. The connections made her eyes widen. "I'm the baby on that card?"

Irene looked at the card and turned it over.

"Aunt Alice is not my aunt? She's my mother?"

"Yes."

"Why am I am only finding this out now? How come she came to visit and didn't stay. How come you made her stay away? Is that why you were always so mean to me? Because I wasn't yours?" Charlotte dumped out a lot of questions, letting what she was feeling pour out. The tears poured down her face.

"The story wasn't mine to tell it was your aunt's. She insisted. In fact, she gave me a letter the day we came to get you. She said I was to give it to you when she passed away. Let me go find it."

Charlotte watched her mother walk into her bedroom. It seemed like she was looking for an escape route. She reviewed the contents of the little cloth bag that she had brought from the island. She opened the locket and looked at the baby face in the picture. Her face.

———

Irene returned after several minutes. She knew exactly where the letter was. She had kept it in the top drawer of her armoire, every day of Charlotte's life. Irene often wondered if she should give the letter to Charlotte before Alice passed away but had honored her promise to Alice. Now she was shaking in anger because Alice had left without warning when all this was not sorted out and mad because the opportunity for both sisters to tell Charlotte the truth had been there, and they had let that chance go.

thirty-seven

. . .

TWENTY-EIGHT YEARS BEFORE.

Alice's head swirled as she sat with pen in hand at the table. What to say, what not to say? She placed her hand on her growing belly and sent warm wishes of happiness to her child. This letter would be the hardest she would ever write.

My dearest child, she began. Her hand reflected the shakiness she was feeling inside.

She mused on what's next. How to explain that this was best for everyone? When she herself didn't believe it. Not one bit. Beatrice would soon arrive, and she needed to get this letter written.

I want you to know I love you with all my heart, with all the love a mother should have for her child. People who loved each other created you, but circumstances have made it impossible for me to raise you myself.

Circumstances being Beatrice, Alice thought. Her mother seemed to take control of every situation, for reasons that were not clear. Alice was many miles away from Beckerville. No one would be aware she was raising a child by herself. No one would even care. But Beatrice would know, and the optics would matter to her.

"Everyone will stare, I will know what they are thinking," Beatrice said when she had arrived in Victoria unexpectedly. "They will know I raised a harlot for a daughter. A daughter who got herself pregnant out of wedlock and is a single parent. No man would want a woman already saddled with someone else's child. You have no hope. This is the best solution."

Alice hadn't known what to do. It was true raising a child on her own would be hard. She knew she could do it. But deep down she also knew she couldn't provide for her baby like another family could. She was old enough for the responsibility. She was twenty-five years old, with a full-time job. It wasn't a question of maturity. It was about providing the best care that a family could provide.

Alice struggled with what was right. She could only provide the baby with the basics. Not a lot of extra money for fun things. Someone else might have more. Especially when that someone else couldn't have children and wanted to. She could see the logic. It hurt her heart to admit it. She had taken many long walks, mulling over the best solution after Beatrice's visit.

Beatrice suggested Irene and Jim could be the baby's parents or, rather, declared they would be. Alice's angst lessened. The baby would stay in the family. She could keep in touch. It would still hurt but having her child with her sister and Jim would be less painful.

"They want to be parents." Beatrice focused on Jim and Irene's needs. "And look Alice, they have a fine home in the country. Country life was good for you, at least until you moved to the big city. Having a child would be the perfect addition to Irene's and Jim's lives. You would help them."

We arranged for your Aunt Irene and Uncle Jim to adopt you. I know you will call them Mother and Dad. They deserve the titles. I know Irene and Jim will give you good care and a good life. I know they will love and support you. I can only hope someday you will still call me Aunt Alice. Even when you know the truth. I am not asking for pity or forgiveness; but I wanted you to know why I gave you away

I guess I should say something about your father. He was like no one I have ever known before—kind, supportive, loving, a friend. All things I didn't expect to find in such a combination in any man, outside of my dad. We fell in love and were planning to marry until the accident. Pete was competing in a sailing race on a day when the weather was bad, lots of wind and enormous waves. I was nervous, but the look in Pete's eye told me he was excited to sail. "Smooth seas do not make a good sailor." He said to me. I kissed him, said I loved him and let him go.

I didn't know about you until a few weeks after his funeral. When you gave your first kick, I thought I had a stomach issue and went for tests. There you were. I still had something of your father, yet you would never know him. I believed it would be just you and me, though and I figured I could manage and tell no one until after you were born.

One day, I ran into your grandma's friend Beth, who lives here in Victoria. She saw how pregnant I was, and despite my request that she not tell my mother, I knew my little plan was in jeopardy. Your grandma arrived two days later and began the steps in a plan I am about to complete tomorrow.

In a red box in my cupboard, you will find some pictures of Pete, so you will know your dad's face. Please do with them as you wish. I kept them for me, to remember happy times, but also to save for you for this day. I asked Irene to keep this letter to give to you on my passing. I didn't want the truth known until I was gone.

I love you very much and hope during the years between writing this letter and you reading it, we get to know each other. I would like that.

Love your mom.

———

Alice called Beatrice only after the baby was born, to ensure Beatrice wouldn't be present for the birth. Having her mother's commanding voice barking orders to anyone while she was in labour would have made it rougher.

"Hello." Beatrice was very brisk on the phone.

"Hi Mother, it's Alice." She tried to make her voice brave and strong, even though it was perhaps the hardest phone call she had ever made.

"It's time?" was Beatrice's only question. No "how are you?"

"She was born this morning."

"Why didn't you call us sooner? It's best if you don't have any time with her."

Alice left the silence to sit. She had no words to argue about what was best. She wanted to tell her mother she didn't call earlier because her mind was on delivering a baby and not calling her mother. But Beatrice would not understand. She understood nothing about Alice.

"Your father and I will be there soon. I'll call you back when I know when. Keep your time with that baby to a minimum. I don't want you getting attached."

Too late, thought Alice as she hung up the phone. She felt blessed she had this time with her daughter before everyone arrived. Before Irene and Jim would become her parents. Alice hugged Charlotte to her chest almost the whole time, hoping the love she felt for the baby would seep into its heart. Charlotte deserved a life with both a mother and a father. Alice knew her own life was much better because of her father's presence. She wanted the same for her daughter. And since Pete wasn't … Alice still had trouble accepting Pete was dead. The accident was five months ago, but he left a large space in her life.

She phoned Irene to put her mind at ease about letting her take Charlotte away. "Hi Irene, it's Alice."

"Alice, how are you? How are you feeling?" Irene was not

her mother in many respects, especially when showing empathy. Alice loved that about her.

"I'm good. I had a little girl this morning."

"Oh, Alice. Are you okay? How did it go?"

Alice shared bare details of the birth, just relaying that everything had gone well and the baby was doing fine.

"What did you name her?" Irene asked.

"Remember our grade two teacher, Miss Webster?"

"She was the best."

"I found out her first name and always loved it. And I gave her Irene as her middle name."

"You named her after me."

"I did. You get to raise her." Alice choked, saying the words.

"Oh, Alice. She will always know you love her."

"Maybe so but she will love you more. And she mustn't know anything. Not until I die. Then she can know the truth. I don't want her confused or to think I did not love her."

"She will never think you don't love her, no matter what. You have my word."

"Mother says they are coming tomorrow. Are you coming with them?"

"We haven't talked about it. I just assumed I was coming. Besides, I don't want Charlotte's first hours to be alone with Momma, she's not very nurturing."

They both laughed.

"Please do. It'll be easier to let her go if you are with her to go back to Beckerville."

"I'll let you know."

The doctor discharged Alice the next day because bottle feeding was going well, and Alice was fine post-delivery. At home, she tucked the baby into bed with her to snuggle together and sleep between feeds. Alice let their days be simple, so Charlotte's life would begin with memories of being loved.

thirty-eight

· · ·

IRENE FOLDED her hands in front of her.

"You didn't have a choice." Charlotte responded with what she thought she heard.

"I didn't have a choice. I think Mother was trying to make it up to me for not allowing me to work out of the home. For getting rid of my dog when she found it digging in her flower beds. For not being able to have children. To make sure that we didn't lose you. She had a cousin who had a baby out of wedlock. She disappeared to have the baby and returned to Beckerville afterwards. No one ever knew where that baby went. The cousin looked for the baby years later but never found the child. I think she eventually died of a broken heart. Momma wasn't going to let that happen to you."

"But how could she think that Aunt Alice would have lost me? She had a job, even though my father was dead, and she could afford to raise me. She was certainly mature enough to look after a child."

"I think Momma was irrational. She thought it made her look bad as a mother if anyone found out Alice wasn't married. She worried someone would find out that you were being raised alone and take you away to foster you somewhere. She didn't trust adoption agencies. They hadn't been very helpful to her cousin, and Momma didn't trust easily. She figured she needed to take precautions. This was her solution. Right or wrong."

"Did you and Aunt Alice ever talk about this when I was growing up?"

"No, not really. Momma forbade us talking about you at all or letting Alice visit. She figured it would confuse you. She worried Alice would want you back one day. After Momma passed away, it was easier because Alice could come visit."

"Would Aunt Alice have taken me back?"

"I don't think so. I think she let you go because she knew your dad and I would take good care of you."

"You did."

"Did we?"

Charlotte looked at her mother's face to understand that question.

Irene explained. "I don't think I was very kind to you all the time. After Momma passed away, Alice came to visit each summer. You loved her. She was adventurous. She knew things I didn't know. I felt threatened. I felt like you loved her more than you loved me. I was worried she would want to take you back to the island with her." Irene looked down at her hands.

Charlotte noticed they were shaking. It was uncomfortable to see her mother so visibly unsure of herself. She didn't know how to respond.

Irene continued. "It bothered me, and I guess I became a little like Momma, a little rash. I told Alice not to come back the next summer. I said that I thought Alice was getting too involved with you. I didn't like it. We argued and didn't talk after that."

"Not at all?"

"She and your dad talked regularly."

"You knew?"

"Of course. I loved your father, but I would never tell him. My generation didn't talk like that. We didn't say those words, they were assumed. But that didn't mean I didn't care. About him or you." Irene continued. "You were a gift that someone else gave to me, entrusted to me. So, I took great care of you. For her. When she started visiting, after Momma died, I saw the happiness in your face. It wasn't a look you had when it was just us. It made me so mad. After all the work I had done to raise you, Alice comes in and makes you shine. So, I told Alice to stay away. I wasn't prepared to have her around every year, making me feel more and more insecure, scared, rejected, not part of the group. I didn't want to lose you. I loved you so much. Just like you were my own."

Charlotte rose to pull the tissue box off the top of the fridge and pushed it in front of her mother. She didn't take one for herself.

"Didn't you know I loved you? I love you?" Irene's lips quivered as she spoke.

"No Mother, I didn't. I couldn't do anything right for you. You didn't let me do the things the other kids my age did. I couldn't figure out what I did wrong. I was a good kid. I helped a lot around the house. I got good grades at school. I couldn't figure out what else I could do to make you happy." Charlotte paused as she let the last sentence fade away. "It's only now that I realize I have been trying to make someone happy. Someone who did not want to be happy. Why mother?" Charlotte searched her mother's face for an answer. "Why don't you want either of us to be happy?"

"I don't know."

"That's not a really kind thing to do to your child."

"No, it's not."

Charlotte got up from the table and picked up her bag. "I'm going home now, Mom."

"Home? Where?"

"To the island. To my home."

"Can I come visit?"

"Do you really want to?" Charlotte walked out the door.

———

The meeting with the lawyer was held in the same room the will was read. Mr. Stoddard got down to business and discussed the various legal requirements to change all of Alice's holdings in the center to Charlotte.

"Of course, none of this happens until you agreed to this," he finished. "You'll see here what she planned in case you declined." Mr. Stoddard handed Charlotte a piece of paper. She stopped reading after the second sentence.

"Something wrong?" Tim asked.

"I just realized I don't need to read this. I will not be declining," Charlotte said and looked at each of the other two men, sure of her choice.

"Well, this is good news," said Tim.

"I agree," said Mr. Stoddard. "Let's get these documents filed and I'll have my assistant call when you need to come in and sign them." He stood up to escort Tim and Charlotte out of the room.

"Tim, do you have time for coffee?"

"How about lunch, it's almost that time and we still have those center files to go through."

"I'd rather just have a chat if that's okay with you. The files can wait."

Tim looked at Charlotte with a puzzled look. "Something the matter?"

"Just some things I want to tell you." Charlotte led them toward the beach walk that she had taken with her aunt each day of her visit. They stopped for tea at the kiosk along the path and then moved to a bench further down. Charlotte sipped her tea and looked at the ocean thinking about how the tide ebbed and flowed no matter what was going on in the world. With Aunt Alice now gone, the world would continue, even though it was slightly altered for her.

"How was your visit to Beckerville?" Tim asked.

"Good. My mother and I were able to clear some things up."

"There were issues between you?"

Charlotte laughed out loud. "You could say that. But listen I didn't ask to chat so you could hear my family woes."

Tim touched her on the arm and held his hand there. "I'm here, if you need to talk."

"I'd like to ask you a question." And when Tim nodded, she said. "Did my aunt ever say anything to you about me?"

"Like what?"

"Did she tell you about me? Did she know what I was like? And how did she know I could run the center?"

"I'm not sure I have the answer to any of that. What I do know is that she was overjoyed when you said you were coming. She told me that you were estranged but not why. And she hoped that it would be the beginning of lots of visits."

"But why did she leave this to me? I can't run the center. I don't know anything about running anything, except spreadsheets."

"I am very certain that your aunt would not have put this on you if she didn't think you could handle it."

"I don't know how she could know that. Aunt Alice and I had two weeks together, how can you be sure about anything in that short of time?"

"Charlotte, your aunt was one of the best judges of character I know. Look at the other women at the center. She handpicked them and they are a team. You get along well with all of them, and they like you. You have business sense. What more do you need?"

"But I was bad at walking dogs, and I can't sail to save my life."

"Hey Charlotte, whoever promised that trying new things would be easy."

"Aunt Alice said first times suck."

Tim laughed. "Sounds like her. What's really bothering you?"

Charlotte looked at Tim with a puzzled frown. "What makes you think something else is bothering me?"

"Intuition. In veterinary medicine the animal comes in with an obvious problem, but you keep checking to make sure that there isn't something else. You make sure you have the root cause. The owner is the one who can tell you more information, and I have found it helps to ask why more than once. So Charlotte, what else is bothering you?"

Charlotte looked at Tim and saw the same compassion her aunt showed her. "I do need to tell you something. Um, where do I start?" Charlotte paused considering how much to tell Tim. "I wasn't sure why my aunt made me pretty much sole heir. I mean, she gave something to her sister, but most of it came to me. I didn't expect that."

"But you are her only heir, besides her sister."

"I know that. But it is more complicated. Turns out I am her daughter."

"Her daughter?" Tim's brows raised in surprise.

"Yes. My father died in a sailing accident and my grandmother didn't think that Aunt Alice could raise me on her own. My grandmother took me to Beckerville and got Irene and Jim to raise me."

"And you only found out now."

"That's the way Aunt Alice, um, my mother wanted it. She wrote me a letter that was to be given to me on her passing."

"And the problem with that is…?"

"No problem. I guess I'm just scared."

"Scared?"

"Scared. What if I mishandle something? What if something happens to one of the dogs and we must bring it to you, to … you know? What happens if we can't make the center run like Aunt Alice did and it must close? I don't want to think she would have been disappointed in me."

"That's all?"

"What do you mean, is that all?"

"I thought it was something serious. Like you had a boyfriend in Beckerville that you didn't want to leave."

"No, nothing like that. I'm just scared."

Tim took Charlotte's empty paper cup and dropped it, with his own, into the garbage can. He took her hand and pulled her to stand up. He tucked her arm into his and held her hand with his other. He guided her down the path. Charlotte leaned into him, and they remained quiet in each other's presence. At the point where the path intersected with the road to her apartment Tim stopped walking.

"I tell you what. I'll make you a promise."

"A promise to what?"

"To give you someone to lean on while you are scared." He bent and kissed her.

thirty-nine

. . .

A MONTH LATER.

"Mom, it's Charlotte."

"Charlotte, it's nice to hear from you. How are things going?"

"Oh, fine Mom. I need you to come to Victoria."

"Why?"

"It's time to spread Aunt Alice's ashes. I want you here with me."

"This is a private thing. Why should I be there? Shouldn't it be between you and your mother?"

"You are my mother, Mom. I want you here to say goodbye."

"Well, it's not convenient for me."

"This is important to me, and Aunt Alice would like it if you were here too."

"Well, this is unexpected. I'm not sure what I can arrange but let me think about it. When did you want to do this?"

"It can happen any time but plan to be here for two days. We need a day to spread the ashes and I'd like a day with you afterwards."

"Sounds like a waste of a time. Why wouldn't you just put

her ashes on a shelf somewhere?" Irene's voice was sharp.

"Mom, I am just doing what she wanted. If you can't see your way to come, then I'll accept that. Can you let me know soon?"

"Fine. I'll call you tomorrow." Irene hung up the phone.

Charlotte looked out at the ocean, wondering why this was so hard for her mom. She decided to call her in an hour or so and ask once more.

"Mom, what's the problem with coming to Victoria?"

"That sister of mine didn't seem to have any respect for anyone else but herself. Imagine, wanting to have your ashes spread."

"What are you upset about?" Charlotte asked.

"It's the expectation that I would want to go to the island and help spread Alice's ashes. I feel a duty, though I don't want to do it."

"There is no duty in this. There is only an ask. Don't make this so hard. You have lost your sister and you need to say your goodbye. Why don't you want to do that?"

"Because you are saying goodbye to your mother. I don't want to be there for that."

"You are my mom. Why are you hanging on to that?"

"I don't know."

"Is it because Alice and I got along?"

"No."

"Because I moved to the island?"

"No."

"Is it because you loved your sister and it's too late to tell her?"

It was like the other end of the conversation was cut off. Then Charlotte heard Irene sniff loudly.

"And to say I am sorry I told her to stay away. That I'm sorry we lost touch."

"Mom."

"Oh Charlotte, this is so hard for me. I feel like an

imposter because I didn't make her important in my life. And now you are making me important in her life. I'm not sure I've earned that regard. I've blamed Momma for everything I have done and took it out on Alice. And you. But I had a choice. I chose the wrong way. And now things are difficult between us. I am so sorry for the way we are together. I don't want to lose you, like I lost Alice."

"You won't Mom." Charlotte paused as something occurred to her. "Have you cried about Aunt Alice passing?"

"No."

"Bout time then."

Irene sniffled.

"You'll come then?"

"I'll let you know when my flight arrives."

———

Flying over the Rocky Mountains, Irene gazed out the window at the landscape below, marveling how, within a couple of hours, the scenery could change from forest and prairie to ocean and mountain. *Remarkable. How can the world change so much in an hour and us humans take so much longer?*

———

Charlotte searched Irene's face for a sign of how she was feeling when she glimpsed her walking down the hallway from the entrance on the airport tarmac. Irene didn't appear upset. Charlotte knew not to trust that too much. She had coached herself to be patient and kind during the visit. She wasn't looking forward to it. But it was the right thing to do. Things were different between them now. They didn't need each other anymore. Now they would choose if they wanted to be together.

"Hello Charlotte." Irene gave her a light hug. Even a light

hug was a big step for Irene. Typically, she did not give hugs at all.

"Hello Mom." Charlotte noted that her mom's head turned quickly and looked at the face that had called her Mom.

Irene smiled a little and Charlotte felt another squeeze. That was foreign to her. Her mother barely ever gave her one hug and now she was getting two.

Something had changed. Perhaps this would be okay.

The day was sunny. Irene stood by the car door while Charlotte set her mother's bag into the back seat. Irene shaded her eyes from the brightness. "Sure, can see why Alice lived here rather than Beckerville."

Charlotte looked at Irene out of the corner of her eye. Soon they were sitting on the deck of the apartment overlooking the water, sipping wine, and watching the water glint and sparkle. "Thank you for coming," Charlotte said for the fourth time.

"Charlotte, it's okay. I am glad I am here. For you."

"There's one thing I have not told you."

"Oh." Irene's eyebrow raised.

"Aunt Alice wanted some of her ashes sprinkled where Pete was lost."

"We have to go on a boat. Into the ocean." squawked Irene.

Charlotte smiled. "On a boat, on to the ocean but the captain is a very good sailor."

"Are you sure it is safe? We won't go overboard like Pete?" Irene continued to squawk.

"It will be just fine. If the weather looks iffy, we won't go, but the forecast is for blue sky and just enough wind. It should be a lovely day."

"I don't know about this."

"Come on Mom, it's time we did something new. This will be a grand adventure.

forty

. . .

THE NEXT DAY Charlotte was grateful for a sunny, warm day, and for calm water. Tim smiled and hugged Charlotte when they arrived at Alice's boat. Charlotte reminded Irene she had met Tim at the funeral.

Tim calmly strapped Irene into a life jacket and instructed her to always have one hand holding the boat. Charlotte noticed Irene grip everything as she moved around to sit down. She thought Tim noticed it too.

"Nothing to worry about, Irene," Tim said. "We will only leave the boat when we can step up to the dinghy."

Irene stood up as if to get off the boat. Then she looked at Tim's face.

Charlotte almost fell overboard when Irene laughed back.

"You were kidding," Irene observed.

"Well not really. It is what we would do, wait until we have to step up to the dingy, but the likelihood is slim. It's a fine day for sailing. Sit back down, Irene." He pointed to a spot in the cockpit near the front. "The wind will bother you less there."

Charlotte shook her head only slightly. She couldn't believe her mother actually laughed at someone's joke.

The ride to the site of the accident was beautiful. The sails fluttered lightly, and the wind gently nudged the boat forward. Water lapped the side of the boat. Cormorants and seagulls followed them. Charlotte closed her eyes, listened to the wind, and smelled the salty air. No doubt this was why her aunt took up sailing and bought a boat. *Make more time for sailing. With Tim.* She thought.

They arrived at the location based on the GPS position taken on the day of the accident. Tim moved some lines connected to the sails and put the motor into neutral. "We'll hove-to here." When he noticed Irene's puzzled look, he added. "That's sailor talk for 'stay right here'."

Charlotte wiped a tear from her eye as she opened the box which held her aunt's ashes. "She wanted half of her ashes spread here. You can help too, Mom, if you like." Her voice was solemn.

Irene moved her hand to the bag and gently lifted out a handful of ash. Without saying a thing, Irene flung the grey particles over the side. They lay on the water and slowly disappeared. She took another scoop that she flung a little further. "Goodbye Alice. Thanks," she said.

Charlotte scooped a handful of her aunt's remains and held them close to her heart. "Thanks, Aunt Alice. For giving me to Mom and then for asking me back when I got older. I am the luckiest girl, I got to have two great moms." She tossed the ashes into the water and blew them a kiss. She repeated with a second handful.

She turned to Tim. "Did you want to spread some?"

"I do."

"Tim, how did you know my sister?" asked Irene.

"I am the vet for the rescue center. Alice and I were great sailing buddies. She taught me how to sail." Tim took a handful of the ash and held it close to his chest and closed his eyes. He took a deep breath and gently sprinkled them off his side of the boat and watched as they drifted with the water.

Irene rose unsteadily on to her feet, to sit beside Charlotte and put her arm around her daughter. "Okay Captain Tim, let's get this boat to shore." Irene said.

"There's more," interrupted Charlotte.

"There's more? What? Are we going to sea?" asked Irene.

"No, we will have lunch at Alice's favorite pub on the water. It's just up island. Captain Tim, you know where."

"Should be there in about thirty minutes."

Charlotte thought about all that had happened to her since her aunt's letter had arrived only a few months before. She would never have this adventure today if it hadn't arrived. Or if she had said no. She wouldn't have visited the island, or learned not to be afraid of dogs, or sailed, or got to know a woman that she loved with all her heart. She now realized she had forgiven Aunt Alice for letting go of her and leaving her with Irene and Jim. They led her here just as much as the invitation did. And Charlotte never would have broken the ice between herself and Irene. She had Aunt Alice to thank for that.

Charlotte reached over to her mom's hands and held them in her own.

"Thanks Mom."

Irene looked like Charlotte had shaken her out of sleep.

"For what?"

"For all this. If you hadn't raised me, this would not be happening today."

Irene blinked twice. Charlotte thought they might be tears but allowed that the wind had blown strands of Irene's hair into her eyes. Irene pulled those strands from across her face and tucked them into the elastic that held her hair.

"If you hadn't come to the island in the first place, I'm not sure we would be here now either." They exchanged a smile.

"Look, Mom," Charlotte pointed to the side of the boat. Seals following their progress to the pub diverted their attention. When the seals saw no food being offered, they splashed away.

Tim directed the boat expertly into the slip and coached the women on their roles to tie it up to the dock. He remained on the boat letting the women go on ahead.

Dino, the pub owner, greeted them at the door. He seated them at a table by the window and took their drink order.

"Don't we get a menu?" Irene asked.

"We are having what they made specially for Aunt Alice."

"What is it?"

"A surprise."

Dino returned with drinks and a plate on a tray for each lady. On each plate was a chicken salad sandwich on sourdough bread, with a large dill pickle and fries.

"Alice Special for you all." He bowed. "Can I get you anything else?"

"No, thanks Dino," said Charlotte. "How are the twins?"

"Very well thank you Charlotte. They are growing so fast and neither of us have had a good sleep for days. But we are blessed."

"Aunt Alice was very fond of them."

"Your aunt was a very special lady. We all adored her. She stopped by here a lot and talked to everyone. Because of her, we found out about this recipe for chicken salad. It's one of our best sellers!" He left them to their meal.

"What's so special about chicken salad?" grumbled Irene. "We are at the ocean. Wouldn't she have wanted seafood?"

"Actually, she was allergic to seafood," said Charlotte. "But she had the best chicken salad recipe. This is it."

"Yum," said Irene, taking her first bite. "Is it curry, and wait, a grape?"

"Yes, isn't it delicious?"

"It is good," said Irene. And they spent a happy half hour eating Alice's favorite sandwich.

"What about Captain Tim?" asked Irene. "Shouldn't he eat too?"

"Dino took his lunch out to him on the boat."

Charlotte called to the owner after they had finished their meal. "Dino, that was delicious, thank you."

"Our pleasure. Now you will come see us sometime, okay?" he hugged Charlotte.

The seagulls cried overhead, mimicking the feeling in Charlotte's heart, but she didn't let the tears fall. Captain Tim was leaning against the railing at the back of the boat, his hat pulled over this face. He rose when he heard them on the dock and asked how their meals were.

"Divine," said Irene. "How was yours?"

"I have always enjoyed coming here with Alice and having that sandwich," he responded. "Let's get underway, we are about forty-five minutes from the center. If you like, I can show you how to sail us there."

He patiently instructed different roles to manage the sails. Charlotte remembered a little of what she learned on her first sailing trip and smiled. Irene's nervousness disappeared only as the dock came into view.

They thanked the captain. Tim gave Charlotte a hug. "See you soon," was all he said.

"Where to now?" asked Irene.

"She wanted some ashes spread along the fence line where she walked dogs every day. But leave some for one more stop."

They sprinkled ashes along the path as they made their way back to the center and the Jetta.

"And now, home."

"You're going to put ashes in her house?"

"Wait and see."

At the apartment, Charlotte stood beside her aunt's Norfolk Pine that lived on the deck. The humidity in the sea breeze provided the extra moisture it needed to stand tall and strong. "Aunt Alice wanted the last of her to rest here so she could always look out at the mountains and the ocean." She gently laid her handful on top of the soil. Irene followed suit. Charlotte used her hands to mix the ashes into the soil, so they would not easily fly away. They stood in silence, acknowledging the solemness of what they had just done.

"How about a glass of wine?" Charlotte offered.

The next day was the most peaceful day Charlotte had ever spent with her mom. They toured the island and ate at Charlotte's favorite places and talked about Aunt Alice and each other. Charlotte asked Irene if she could stay longer.

"I've got a job." Irene looked proud of her announcement.

"A job? Doing what?"

"You remember how everyone at the care facility raved about the food I brought in sometimes for your father?"

"Yes."

"Well, their cook retired, and they called and asked if I would be interested."

"Well, look at you. I'm happy for you."

"Me too. I've been there two weeks now. It's busy but I am loving it. I promise I'll come back to the island soon, and often."

———

Charlotte hugged her mother at the departures gate, feeling that the Victoria tradition of hugs would be a habit for them. "Here Mom, this is for you. I thought you might like it."

Irene held the small porcelain jar with a lid. It was navy blue with yellow flowers painted and fit perfectly in her hand.

"Was this one of Alice's?" she asked.

"No, it is some of Alice. I thought you might like some of her ashes to take back with you."

Irene's eyes teared. "Thank you, Charlotte. I love you."

"I love you too, Mom."

Down the hallway to the waiting area, Irene turned, blew a kiss to her daughter, and waved goodbye.

As Charlotte walked to her car, her cell phone rang. The display read "Tim" and her heart soared.

———

acknowledgments

As with all big projects there are many hands that made this book what it is.

Over the years I have taken courses and belonged to writing groups that grew my skills. Alexandra Writers' Centre Society has been a special place to spend time to learn, share, and improve. I have been grateful to be a member there.

Without the Bestseller Experiment and the work of Mark Stay and Mark Desvaux, I doubt this book would be online. I started listening to their podcast when it began in 2016 and have enjoyed every episode since. The podcasts have been so rich in perspective, ideas, and considerations in the art and science of writing. I signed up for the Academy for a year to help me achieve my goal of publishing. While I missed my original deadline by a few months, I still got it done. Thanks, the 2 Marks. I wouldn't be writing this without your contribution to the writing world.

Without the help of Teresa and Bonnie, this story wouldn't have the depth their input provided. They read it first after me and helped evolve the story further than I could alone. Any mistakes in this book are my own.

My cheer squad kept me at the desk writing and editing by asking how my book was coming often enough that I pushed it to the finish line rather than admit I couldn't. In no defined order they are Renee, Lori, Maureen, Janet, Lana, Shian, Sandy, Allison, June, and Joann. Thanks to you all for your support.

about the author

Barb Reimer began writing as cathartic work to move thoughts, worries, and ideas to paper and out of her head. When cobbled together some of them became stories about relationships between women of all ages.

She honed her craft with organizations like the Alexander Writer's Center at www.alexandrawriters.org and The Best-Seller Academy at www.Bestsellerexperiment.com. Both provided learning and support. She is grateful to them for their impact on her skills and the way she thinks about writing.

All of this, the encouragement from friends, and a pile of drafts led to *A Mother's Gift*, Barb's first novel.

She is working on another story about women and their relationships with each other. *A Mother's Treasure* will be published in early 2023. These woman also come from Beckerville, the setting for *A Mothers' Gift*. Seems the town of Beckerville has more than one set of female relationships that have a story behind them.

Barb's blog and other creative efforts can be found at www.barbreimer.ca.

www.ingramcontent.com/pod-product-compliance
Lightning Source LLC
Chambersburg PA
CBHW061203210726
48294CB00006B/1734